Up Goes the Curtain

Books By Janet Lambert

PENNY PARRISH STORIES
Star Spangled Summer 1941
Dreams of Glory 1942
Glory Be! 1943
Up Goes the Curtain 1946
Practically Perfect 1947
The Reluctant Heart 1950

TIPPY PARRISH STORIES
Miss Tippy 1948
Little Miss Atlas 1949
Miss America 1951
Don't Cry Little Girl 1952
Rainbow After Rain 1953
Welcome Home, Mrs. Jordon 1953
Song in Their Hearts 1956
Here's Marny 1969

JORDON STORIES
Just Jennifer 1945
Friday's Child 1947
Confusion by Cupid 1950
A Dream for Susan 1954
Love Taps Gently 1955
Myself & I 1957
The Stars Hang High 1960
Wedding Bells 1961
A Bright Tomorrow 1965

PARRI MACDONALD STORIES
Introducing Parri 1962
That's My Girl 1964
Stagestruck Parri 1966
My Davy 1968

CANDY KANE STORIES
Candy Kane 1943
Whoa, Matilda 1944
One for the Money 1946

DRIA MEREDITH STORIES
Star Dream 1951
Summer for Seven 1952
High Hurdles 1955

CAMPBELL STORIES
The Precious Days 1957
For Each Other 1959
Forever and Ever 1961
Five's a Crowd 1963
First of All 1966
The Odd Ones 1969

SUGAR BRADLEY STORIES
Sweet as Sugar 1967
Hi, Neighbor 1968

CHRISTIE DRAYTON STORIES
Where the Heart Is 1948
Treasure Trouble 1949

PATTY AND GINGER STORIES
We're Going Steady 1958
Boy Wanted 1959
Spring Fever 1960
Summer Madness 1962
Extra Special 1963
On Her Own 1964

CINDA HOLLISTER STORIES
Cinda 1954
Fly Away Cinda 1956
Big Deal 1958
Triple Trouble 1965
Love to Spare 1967

UP GOES
THE CURTAIN

BY

JANET LAMBERT

Image Cascade Publishing
www.ImageCascade.com

MANUFACTURED IN THE UNITED STATES
OF AMERICA

A hardcover edition of this book was originally published by
E. P. Dutton & Co. It is here reprinted by arrangement with
Mrs. Jeanne Ann Vanderhoef.

First *Image Cascade Publishing* edition published 2001.
Copyright renewed © 1974 by Jeanne Ann Vanderhoef.

Library of Congress Cataloging in Publication Data
Lambert, Janet, 1895–1973.
        Up goes the curtain.

(Juvenile Girls)
Reprint. Originally published: New York: E. P. Dutton,
1946.

ISBN 978-1-930009-29-5

Dear Readers:

    Mother always said she wanted her books to be good enough to be found in someone's attic!

    After all of these years, I find her stories—not in attics at all—but prominent in fans' bookcases just as mine are. It is so heart-warming to know that through these republications she will go on telling good stories and being there for her "girls," some of whom find no other place to turn.

        With a heart full of love and pride–
        Janet Lambert's daughter,
          Jeanne Ann Vanderhoef

To Frances

Up Goes the Curtain

CHAPTER I

ALL THE stools before the soda fountain were empty, and the waitress on duty straightened from setting freshly washed glasses on a shelf under the counter, and stretched her aching back. She lifted one tired foot, then the other, hoping for a moment's rest, and sighed as she watched two figures sprinting in the door.

"I'll bet myself a double coke that the old gal gets here first," she muttered, as a fat woman blocked a pretty, hurrying girl by swinging an umbrella and two overloaded market baskets. But the girl side-stepped neatly, and, with quick light steps, had almost reached one of the red leather stools, when her competitor put on a burst of speed and bustled in ahead of her. The waitress sighed, for she had lost several wagers with herself that day, and as she leaned forward to take the order, she watched the girl slide on to a stool around the bend of the counter.

My, she's pretty, the waitress thought enviously, half-listening to instructions in sandwich-making and a whining plea for butter. And rich, too. I wish I had a fur jacket like that, real honest-to-goodness fur.

The girl had taken off her gloves. She had opened her lynx jacket and was staring solemnly at herself in the mirror behind the counter, her eyebrows drawn a little together, her soft lips puckered. "Penny Parrish," she said suddenly to her reflected self, "you're a fool."

"Do you want something, miss?"

9

"Hm? Oh, I'm sorry. I'd like a coke, please."

The waitress watched the girl's eyes light up, a soft, rich brown, with dancing lights in them that matched her bronze bell of hair. Her head tipped to one side and she smiled shyly and apologetically.

"I have a frightful habit of talking to myself," she said. "Do you ever do it?"

"Sure. Large coke, or small?"

"Large, I think—and with lots of ice, if you can spare it."

"Sure."

The girl, who had called herself Penny, watched while syrup was squirted into a glass, followed by a hiss of charged water, the two being adroitly blended with a clinking spoon. "You don't waste a single motion," she said, when the glass was set before her. "I'll bet it's fun, isn't it?"

"It was at first. Now, it's a headache." The waitress reached for a container of straws, less grudgingly than when she had slammed the fat woman's sandwich before her, and when she pushed back a straggling lock of yellow hair, looked almost as young as she really was.

"Have you worked here long?" Penny asked.

"Six months."

"I've been in New York six months. I—I'm an actress."

"You are? I thought you were a debutante out slumming. Movies?"

"No. I suppose I shouldn't quite say that I'm an actress, yet. I was in a sort of stock company last summer, training, you know, and I've been wearing my shoes out all winter, trying to get a job. But now I have a part in a Broadway play."

"Then I don't see why you called yourself a fool. It looks to me as if you're doing all right."

"Oh, I am. But you see. . . ." Penny took a sip of her drink, then pushed the glass aside. "I'm all alone here and I'm sort of homesick."

"That's tough. No family, huh?"

"Oh, yes, loads of family. But they're all out at Fort Knox, Kentucky. My father's an army officer."

"Well, I guess we've all got somebody in the war."

"Have you?"

"A husband."

"Oh, that's too bad."

The waitress had picked up a cloth and was washing the counter, but she stopped to ring the cash register and flip the fat woman a check. "He's been overseas almost a year," she said, beginning to wipe again.

"In what branch of the service?"

"Foot soldier. And no one ever hated to walk worse than Joe."

Penny, on her stool, laughed. There was nothing she enjoyed so much as talking with people; not to them, about them, but with them. She forgot she was homesick, forgot to drink her coke, but sat with her elbow on the porcelain counter, her soft round chin cupped in the palm of her hand, listening to the story of Joe and a girl he called Letty.

"So you see," Letty ended, aiming the wet cloth unerringly at a basin of water and sending a great deal of her pent-up emotion with it, "I never could live out in Jamaica with Joe's mom and the kids. They'd drive me crazy and take all my money."

"So you just stay in town and work, to save your allotment. I think it's marvelous of you." Penny's eyes glowed with admiration, but Letty only shrugged it away and took her turn at polite questioning.

"It's different with you," she said. "Gee, if you've got a home and are so lonesome, why don't you go back to it? You looked ready to cry when you came in."

"Well," Penny crossed one slim leg over the other, anchored a heel over a rung on the stool, and settled herself as though she had found a very pleasant place to be and intended to stay awhile... "It's like this," she explained. "Last year, on my eighteenth birthday, I made a solemn vow with myself that I'd succeed, and I have to stick to it. I can go home after the play closes and not feel that I've failed. But the trouble is, Janice Ware's in the play—and she's so wonderful that it's sure to be a hit. It may be ages before I'll get home."

"And in the meantime, you have to stay here alone, huh?"

"Well, not exactly alone. My sister-in-law used to be my best friend long before she married my brother. Now she's out at Fort Knox with him, and I live here in her apartment."

"Wait till I see what the guy up the line wants."

Letty swished along her narrow runway and Penny pulled her coke back to her. She wondered how she could explain loneliness in a triplex apartment on Park Avenue, with a wide terrace overlooking the lights and life of New York, and six servants. She hadn't dreamed it could happen when she moved her possessions into the rose bedroom she had shared so often with Carrol, but it had happened. And Penny, who needed companionship as a bright flower needs its stem, was alone with only a butler to talk to, or the maids, or faded Miss Turner, who had been Carrol's governess and now acted as Penny's chaperon. So, when Letty came back, she began carefully:

"Carrol's father died and left her an awful lot of money . . . millions, really, and I simply adored him. I called him Uncle Lang, and loved him next to Mums and Dad. So when she and David . . ."

"Wait a minute." Letty laid both elbows on the counter and rested on them. She was enjoying this more than a magazine serial, read in her shabby room under a swinging light bulb, but the story began in the middle. So she said, "Who's Carrol, and who's David, and where are they?"

"Why, David's my brother and Carrol's my best friend, and they're married. After Uncle Lang died last year, Carrol hadn't another relative in the world. So, when David graduated from West Point they were married and went out to Fort Knox."

"Out where your mother and father are?"

"Umhum. But they weren't there, then."

"Oh, gosh." Letty sighed and went off to slide a cup under the spigot of a coffee urn, and Penny laughed.

It all seemed so simple to her. She was accustomed to a family that had moved about in the regular army, long before she was born. She saw nothing odd in a father's being transferred from the cavalry to the armored force, and arriving on a post to find his son and new daughter-in-law already there. Things like that were always happening in the army. And younger brothers, like Bobby, were whisked out of one military school and into one nearer home, without so much loss as the parsing of a sentence. And very small sisters, the size of Tippy, played dolls again with little girls they had once bashed over the head with a rattle. And Mums and other mothers found new spots for the same old furniture; then went marketing in a Post Exchange that looked like dozens of other Post Exchanges. When the furniture was in place, people began dropping in and saying, "Good gracious, how the children have grown since we were together in the Philippines . . . or Panama . . . or Fort Mead, South Dakota."

That was the way the army had always been; but now, in wartime, it was a little more complicated. Officers were ordered overseas. They said good-by to their families, just as Letty's Joe had done, and the families stored their belongings and tried to become civilians. That had happened to the Parrishes last year when Colonel Parrish flew off to England. But now they were reunited again at Fort Knox, and Penny knew how precious and fleeting the months were, or it might be even the days. She tried to explain it to Letty, at interrupted intervals, and ended by saying:

"And that's why Carrol keeps her apartment; so we'll have a place to live when Dad and David have to go. For they will have to go, you know, and I'll feel *awful* if I haven't been with them."

"Sure, I know how I'd feel if it was me. If Mom and Pop were still out in Iowa, you can bet I wouldn't be here, grubbing along alone."

"But I just got this today." Penny opened her purse and took out a rolled-up manuscript. It was clamped inside a blue paper cover, and she laid it on the counter, enjoying its thickness. "It's a wonderful part," she sighed, patting it. "It's my big chance."

"Gee, it does look good." Letty pulled the manuscript to her and began leafing through it. "You've got an awful lot to learn," she said, scanning the pages. "How soon do you have to know it all?"

"Rehearsals won't start for three weeks. They haven't finished casting yet, but Miss Ware chose me early because I'm a friend of hers and was in the stock company she owns."

"Well then, why don't you go out to Fort Knox while you wait?"

Penny's eyes met Letty's for an instant. Brown and blue stared into each other, and Penny was the first to give a gasp of excitement. "Oh, my!" she cried, "I think I'll do it! I'll go home for three weeks!"

"Can you?"

"I hope so. I'll telephone Miss Ware tonight and ask her. Oh, Letty. . . ." She reached across and clutched Letty's hands that still held the typewritten part. "How can I ever thank you? How can I ever do half as much for you as you've done for me? I was so awfully low. . . ."

"Pooh, I haven't done a thing you wouldn't have thought of by yourself, after awhile; and I've had fun, too."

"Have you, Letty?" Penny was sliding forward on her stool in her eagerness. "Could you come home to dinner with me?" she asked," so we could talk more about things and kind of plan for both of us?"

But Letty shook her head. "I can't, really. I'm on here until ten," she answered, suddenly remembering the manager at the cigar counter, and looking across to find him frowning at her. "Things are going to get busy from now on and I guess you'd better go."

"But will you still be here when I come back from Knox?"

"Sure. I've been here for six months and I guess I can stand it three weeks longer."

"And we'll do something together. We'll have dinner on your night off. Will you?"

"That'd be swell."

"Then don't forget." Penny crammed the manuscript back into her purse and held out her hand. "Don't forget, Letty, will you?" she urged. "I'll be back here three weeks from today to find you. Now, remember."

"I'll remember."

"We're friends, so tell Joe about it." Penny's lips were smiling and she gave Letty's hand a hard little squeeze. "We'll have lots to talk about," she promised, "when I come back!"

She laid her check and nickel before the cashier, sent a wave of her hand back to Letty, and felt as if her feet were too light to carry her along the pavement.

It was so pleasant outside with the first hint of spring in the March air. Women were wearing gay flowers on their hats that looked as if a pale sun had brought a garden to bloom on their heads, and Penny smiled to herself as she breezed along, wondering if people noticed that she floated an inch or two from the ground, like a happy balloon. She chose a cross street at random, and was taking the long blocks from Broadway to Park Avenue without being aware of it, when a restaurant window brought her up short. It was filled with ice on which fish and oysters were temptingly displayed, and Penny whisked across the sidewalk to stand before it.

Why, this is the way I came home last year when I was so unhappy and sure I wouldn't ever be a success, she thought, silently addressing a large red lobster in the middle of the window. And you look like the same fellow who was here then.

She stood looking down through the glass, remembering the night she had dined with Miss Ware, a young eager girl, with her hopes and dreams in her eyes; and with words ready to float from her lips like bright bubbles. But Terry Hayes had stolen her dreams and shattered the bubble pipe of her ego. As a helpful friend, but also as a young officer possessed of too much charm, he had squeezed himself in at their table for two, and had proceeded to interest Miss Ware in himself while Penny sat in hopeless, silent misery.

"The great Terry Hayes," she laughed now, walking on more slowly and letting her mind wander through the past year, from the time her father had been stationed at West Point and she had turned from the thrill of cadet hops to the drudgery that was hidden behind the shine of footlights. She let it dwell tenderly on the fun she had had, the sorrow, the work, and her thoughts carried her into a tall apartment building and up in a swiftly silent elevator.

There was richness even upon the satiny brown wood of the little cage, and Penny realized how quickly she had become accustomed to luxury. Once she had been round-eyed with awe when the doors slid open, and had come slowly out, treading softly, and wondering a little at the great hall, the thick carpets, the maze of rooms and stairways. Now she gave her hat and coat to Perkins, as casually as Carrol would do, and answered the gentle voice of Miss Turner who was calling from the drawing room:

"Penny, darling, is that you?"

"In person." Penny stood in the door and looked down the long room to the little woman who filled only a small portion of an overstuffed chair. "I got the part," she announced, tossing back her hair and grinning, "and I think I can go out to Fort Knox for three weeks."

"How lovely to both announcements. Oh, Penny, I'm so happy for you!"

"I am, too." Penny danced over the carpet to smooth Miss Turner's silvery hair and to drop a kiss on her soft white cheek. "Of course, I'll have to ask Miss Ware if I may go," she said, "but I think she'll let me. I'll whip into the library and call her now. Then I'll come back and tell you all about it."

She was quite breathless from excitement when Janice Ware's full, throaty voice came to her over the telephone, for even though she had proved herself to be a clever in-génue, capable of handling a part in a New York opening, Penny still felt very young when she had the good fortune so much as to gaze upon a veteran of the theater. She was like a little girl in the presence of august and royal personages, and while she managed to control her knees from dipping in curtsies, her voice made a series of them, until actors like old Mr. Farthingham, who was grouchy and tired but world-famous, cleared his throat and remarked grudgingly, "A very charming child."

"Of course you may go, Penny," Miss Ware said, so promptly and gladly that Penny's taut shoulders relaxed and she shut her eyes so as to give the delightful sound in her ear no peephole of escape. "Rehearsals will start the fifth of April, and if you're even a day or two late it won't matter so much."

"Oh, I'll be back on time. I wouldn't miss the first few minutes of excitement for the world." Penny wanted to kiss the receiver, but somehow she managed a sedate, "Thank you and good-by" before she flung her arms over her head and let out an exultant whoop.

"This is my lucky day," she sang, just as the telephone rang again. She sat up very straight to answer it, but when the first words came over the wire, she leaned back in the red leather chair which held her, propped her feet on the desk, and slid down on her spine.

"Terry Hayes!" she cried. "I was just thinking of you this afternoon. For goodness' sake, where are you?"

"At Fort Dix. I got in from England the other day and thought I'd give you a ring while I'm taking myself a breather. How's everything?"

"Fine." Penny could visualize young Major Hayes taking his "breather" wherever he happened to be; in the uphol-stered comfort of the Officers Club, or prone upon a bed in his temporary barracks. He was undoubtedly as comfortable

as she was, so she slid still lower in her chair and prepared
herself for one of their usual, lengthy chats. But after a few
sentences he asked abruptly:

"Where's that brother of yours? Still at Knox?"

"Umhum, and Dad and Mother are there."

"Swell. I'm going out and I want to have a talk with
Dave."

"Why, *Terry!*" Penny grinned gleefully. "I'm going out,
too. We can have a regular reunion, can't we?"

There was a second's pause, long enough for Penny to
wait with a puzzled frown until he answered casually, "That
will be fine, Pen. I'll see you there. When are you leaving?"

"I don't know. I haven't a reservation, yet."

"Well, I'm hopping off tomorrow. My trip's one of those
spur-of-the-moment affairs, and I want to be sure to reach
Dave. Will care of his division do it?"

"Yes." Penny wished for television. The voice was
Terry's; but the clipped sentences, the strange hesitations,
didn't match his blue eyes that always seemed to be laughing
at her, or his wide grin, or the way he cocked his head on
one side when he teased her. He was Terry—and yet he
wasn't. And to make him even stranger, he listened to the
operator say, "Your three minutes are up, sir," then said a
quick good-by, and hung up.

"Well!" Penny sat staring at the telephone for some time.
Where were the gay remarks about marriage? The deluge
of books and flowers? The "I love you's" that had followed
her as she toiled up the steps in the Statue of Liberty, or the
compliments that made people turn their heads in the theater
and issue a warning "Sh!" Terry could pout and be cross, or

he could grin and poke fun at her; he could even disappear from her life for months and then turn up for another battle of wits; but never before had he used this cold voice that could air-condition a room.

Penny felt abandoned, sitting alone in the library. She liked Terry; sometimes she even wondered if she weren't a little in love with him. And she forgot her part in the play while she worried over this new turn in her affairs. Being Penny was a complex business, and as a single thought could engage her completely, and for a very long time, it was quite dark in the library before she snapped on a light, pulled out the thick telephone directory, and looked up the number of the Pennsylvania station.

CHAPTER II

THE TRIP to Fort Knox was so eventful to Penny that in the sober trainload of passengers she was like a small comet, loose from its moorings, and happily disporting itself through the neat pattern of things.

To begin with, she was late in reaching the station. A last-minute cancellation had put her on the train eighteen hours after she had asked for a reservation, and hurried packing had necessitated more bags than she could successfully manage. The reservation was for a bedroom as far as Pittsburgh, with a transfer into a berth to Louisville; and she was jubilant.

"I might just as well go in style," she said to Miss Turner, who was trying to bring order into a hand-trunk that had been packed with utter disregard for hangers. "Goodness knows, it's more than I can afford; but Terry Hayes may be on this train and I'll look simply elegant sitting in a little room that has a door on it."

But once she was in the little room, when the porter had found hiding places for the impedimenta of her visit, she put her hat and coat in the small closet, tried all the electrical fixtures, and then popped out into the corridor again. In the open part of the car where there would be curtain-hung berths at night, a young mother was having trouble with a crying baby and a pink and white basket. So Penny held the baby while the mother made up his bed again. They chatted for a few moments until Penny, feeling she must get full value-received for her money, reluctantly returned to her private room. There she sat, watching the outlying wastes of Newark sweep past, feeling excited and adventurous, but also lonely; as the really rich often are lonely in the fine privacy their money can buy.

The train sped out of Newark and was on its way to Philadelphia when Penny decided she might be hungry. She brushed her shining bright brown hair again, hastily dabbed a smudge of powder on her nose, and was standing in her doorway when she saw Terry Hayes swinging along the corridor.

"Hi," she called, watching him grasp the brass rail as the train rounded a curve, "I sort of thought you'd be here."

"Penny, by all that's holy!"

He looked very tall and broad-shouldered, standing in the low, narrow hallway. His uniform fitted him in true custom-made fashion that was further enhanced by three service ribbons; and smiling and glad to see him, Penny stepped back from the door and invited:

"Come in and relax. As the spider said, 'My parlor isn't very large, but....'"

"How did you happen to catch this train?" Terry stayed with one hand resting against the doorframe, and Penny stopped looking up at him and sat down suddenly.

It seemed an odd greeting from a man you hadn't seen for three months, especially from a man who took his courtship like a track runner takes hurdles, and her head went a little higher than usual as she answered, "Because I was given a reservation on it. Does it matter?"

"No, I just wondered."

Up Goes the Curtain

He came in and sat beside her, and the strange shadowy Terry, who was no one she could touch or understand, came in, too, and sat down like a ghost between them. For almost an hour Penny fought through the Tunisian campaign; was flown back and forth across the Atlantic like a commuter between the United States and England; was blitzed in London; missed a connection in Lincoln, Nebraska, and bore it all with a steady smile. But when she found herself in the technical business of building a tank, she struggled up through the armored plating and rivets to suggest with spirit:

"Listen, I'm not going to fight in one of those contraptions, so I don't need to learn how to find its triggers and gears and switches blindfolded. And besides, I'll see plenty of them at Knox."

Terry sighed and agreed. "I suppose so. How long are you planning to stay?"

"Three weeks."

She turned ever so little to watch him, but he only leaned his head against the white Pullman towel on the back of the seat and considered the mirror across from him. So many inches across, his eyes counted, so many inches down, so many square inches therein; until Penny wanted to snap her fingers under his fine straight nose and bring him up out of his trance. "I'm hungry," she said suddenly, standing up and brushing the wrinkles out of her beige wool dress. "Would'st eat?"

Terry sat up at that. He looked at her with an appealing and boyish apology that was another facet in his diamond of charm, and said ruefully, "I'm awfully sorry, Pen. There's another gal on the train. I've got a date with her for lunch."

"Oh." Penny felt a small blush rising, but she turned her back and scrubbed it off with powder. "In that case," she said lightly, "I hope you won't mind if I leave you. It's been a long time since breakfast."

"Would you like to go in with us?"

"No, thanks." She opened the closet door and took out her lynx jacket, inspecting it carefully as though it might have caught moths during its brief incarceration, then slid into it before Terry could rise and hold out his hand. "I'll see you at Fort Knox," she said from the door. "Drop in whenever you feel like it, or at David and Carrol's. Some of us will always be around."

"Pen?"

"Yes?" She turned suddenly and they both got wedged in the door.

"I'm sorry about lunch," Terry said. "If I'd known you'd be on the train, I...." And then he sighed and straightened his shoulders. "I guess it wouldn't have made much difference," he added. "I might as well tell you—I'm dated up for dinner, too. But could I come in and talk with you this evening?"

"What about? Not your part in the war again, I hope." Penny's little chin rose out of its circle of fur and he thought how cute it looked, reaching for a place that wasn't as high as the world his necktie lived in.

"No. About your play, perhaps. We—I—I haven't given you much chance to talk about that. And then . . ." he stopped, waited a moment, and said slowly, "I'm an assistant G2 at Fort Dix, you know."

26

Up Goes the Curtain

"Yes, so I heard." G2 meant nothing to Penny. Her father had been G2 of something-or-other one time, and except for the fact that he was on a general's staff, she had given it little thought. So she said, "Drop in if you care to, although I have to move into a Louisville car at nine-thirty." Then she turned away, sent back a casual wave of her hand, and lurched with dignity along the swaying corridor.

Hm, she thought, struggling with the outer door and then the clanking vestibule, I'll never again believe anything the great Hayes puts out. He's a—a worm in wolf's clothing.

With each car she traversed, with each door she shoved open, she became more indignant. And when the dining car steward seated her at a table with two sailors and a small meek man who scribbled on a scratch pad while he ate, she kept her eyes on the menu and refused to let herself watch for Terry and the "gal" he was bringing to lunch. After she had ordered, she played a game with herself, counting animals in the fields that flashed past, and wiping out her score whenever she saw a cemetery. The little man went off with his notebook, the sailors finished their meal and pushed back their chairs, and, as she let her eyes swing up to them, a too familiar voice said:

"Why, Penny Parrish, by all that's holy!" And there stood Terry, beaming down at her, eye-crinkles and grin, and with him a fashion-magazine girl who looked as if she had been cut out and pasted against him. Penny saw black hair, very smooth in an ultra-smart upsweep, topped by a bit of black felt with a caressing are of coke feathers which cradled a cheek; long gray eyes and a red, red mouth. A girl so unlike the fresh youthfulness of Penny that the steward was obsequiously twitching out chairs at a table for two.

"We'll sit here if you don't mind, Pen," Terry said, lifting her limp hand from the table in a vigorous shake. "This is Marcia McMain, Penny Parrish. I gather, from you're being on this train with the family at Knox, that we're all going to the same place. Right?"

"Right." Penny nodded dazedly and watched Marcia sink into the chair Terry held for her. She didn't sit, the movement was too fluid for that, and Penny suddenly thought of a fuzzy black caterpillar she once had watched. The caterpillar had the same boneless grace of Marcia, but they both got around very well. She almost smiled, thinking how idiotic it was to let her mind wander at a time like this, and Terry accepted the flicker as one of conspiracy. He began to shower her with personal and pointed questions, and at last pushed his plate aside to rest his elbows on the table.

"So good old David's out there," he said, as if she hadn't already told him. "I'm hoping he'll show me all the new armored stuff. The secret hard-to-find-out-about stuff," he added, turning to Marcia. "They test everything at Fort Knox." And then he explained to Penny, "Marcia has an uncle living in Louisville. When I told her I had to make this inspection trip she thought she'd come along for a visit."

"That's nice." Penny smiled and signaled for her check. "I hope you'll come see us," she said, in the stiff manner of a child who has been taught to be polite but means nothing it says.

"Thank you," Marcia's red lips parted then closed, without leaving a trace of having spoken. Not a feature on her face was disarranged. Her lips were simply double-doors that opened to let a few words come out, then shut, and stayed shut until it was time for them to open again.

She watched Penny leave the dining car and for a moment Terry watched her too. Then he turned sidewise in his chair, grinned his impudent grin and winked. "You and I are going to have a swell time at Knox," he said.

Back in her room, Penny got out her part in the play. She closed her door tightly and settled down to learn her lines. *The Robin's Nest* had sounded like a wonderful play the evening Miss Ware had read it to her; but struggling with the sentences that ended "X right" or "Business with tea tray," she wondered how much of it had been the pure timbre of Miss Ware's voice or her red-gold hair under the lamplight. The thing was stupid. She laid the manuscript on the seat beside her and stared down at it. How could any play be a hit that had for an ingénue's opening speech, "I came because I . . . because I . . . because I . . . ?" Pooh, she thought. Every time the author couldn't think of a way to end a speech he put down a string of little dots and wrote "exit." Tears gathered on Penny's lashes. She could see herself failing. For even though the author was unable to express his characters' feelings, she would be supposed to drag out meaning that wasn't there.

She was to breathe life into a stupid girl who either jumped about or fiddled; who was tied up in emotional but inarticulate knots; and who either rattled on like an old Ford or fizzled out like a wet firecracker. She couldn't do it. She would fail. On opening night people would rustle their programs and sigh; the newspapers would pity her; Terry, sitting somewhere in the first few rows, would turn to the ultra-smart Marcia beside him and murmur, "Poor kid, let's give her ten points for effort." In desperation she began counting cows and sheep again, and, at last, her eyes blurred from staring at brown fields, brown hills, brown trees, she tucked her feet under her, leaned her head against the corner of the seat, and slept.

The train rushed on. It clattered across Pennsylvania with its whistle blowing and its smoke and cinders settling on people in the hills as if shouting to them that it was giving back what remained of the coal they had dug. "Th-a-n-k-s," the whistle said. "Th-a-n-k-s."

Penny opened her eyes and uncurled herself. It was dusk in her small room, and she reached for a light switch that flooded everything with a soft golden glow. Then she turned on all the lamps and bulbs she could find, and the little place became warm and cozy. Her play still lay on the seat and she picked it up. She read her opening line softly, looking across at the handle on a cabinet but seeing Miss Ware.

"I came because I. . . ." Her lower lip drew in tightly, pulling a little breath with it. "Because I. . . ." Her breath was caught and couldn't be released. "Because I. . . ." The breath went out of her. There were no more words—nothing more would come. The author had known that; he had sat at his desk and watched her; had waited for her eyes to drop before he let someone walk across the room to help her.

Oh, it was a wonderful part!

Penny forgot the time. A waiter went along the corridor saying, "Last call for dinner, last call for dinner," and at last the porter rang the bell on her door and told her:

Up Goes the Curtain

"It's Pittsburgh, miss. Want me to change your bags now?"

"Oh—oh, yes," she answered, not as Penny, but as Drucilla in *The Robin's Nest*. "Please."

She forgot to look for Terry when she followed the porter, for she was still Drucilla, stumbling a little in shy awkwardness. And she stayed Drucilla while she pinned up her hair on bobby-pins. The green curtains of her berth shut her into a wonderful stage, and she touched her cold cream jar, her cleansing tissue and comb, with hesitant fingers. Sometimes she stared dreamily at herself in the small mirror between the windows; sometimes she clattered and spilled things; and sometimes she talked to herself, not using the author's lines, but her own, in the way Drucilla would speak.

"Oh me," she sighed at last, flipping off the light and snuggling down under the heavy Pullman blanket, "I do lead the most divine life. I guess I'll lie here and think about it awhile."

But again the train lulled her, and light was coming from under the drawn shades when she heard a hand go thump-thump against the curtains and an urgent voice say through a slit in them, "Louisville, miss. Louisville, in half an hour."

Penny struggled into her clothes like a wrestler practicing the scissor-hold or a headlock, and staggered to the dressing-room with her toilet case. There was no sign of Terry or the beautiful Marcia, but when the train had pulled into the station sheds and she was following an undersized Red Cap with her oversized bags, wondering when or where one found a bus to Fort Knox, she saw them saying good-by.

The tracks ran close to the street, separated from it by

only a high picket fence, and Marcia was entering a taxi while a soldier put Terry's army kit and meusette bag into a waiting government car. The taxi slid away from the curb and Penny sent a half-hearted wave after it that changed to a ride-thumbing motion as Terry turned toward her. "Give me a lift, mister?" she called.

"Sure." Terry hurried across the sidewalk to the gates and relieved her of her hat box and toilet case. "Won't the family be in to meet you?" he asked.

"I didn't tell them I'm coming. I want it to be a surprise."

"Well, in that case, we'll break an army regulation about civilians riding in government cars. Hop in."

Penny lost no time in scrambling across the brown leather seat. "This is a break," she said to the soldier who was piling her bags in front, "and it's making me feel as if I'd come home. I just want to pat everything because it looks so *army*."

She chattered all the thirty-five miles to the post, catching up on her gossip with Terry, speaking gayly of Marcia and of all the plans they would make. But when they reached the sentry box and a guard came out to question them, she sat forward and pressed her face against the glass.

"That's Goldville, over there," Terry said, pointing to street after street of frame apartment houses. "Is that where Carrol and David live?"

"Oh, mercy, no." Penny laughed and looked back to watch Goldville disappear around a curve. "They have what David describes as a wooden shack in a place called Angel Alley. Doesn't that sound divine? Carrol calls it 'a simply darling bungalow'—but I'll bank on David."

"Imagine that for the rich ex-Miss Houghton. Does she mind?"

"She thinks it's super." A traffic light halted them and Penny looked at the criss-cross of streets it controlled. "Goodness," she said, "the post is as big as a town."

The car turned into a section of red brick houses that edged the parade ground, and she took a deep breath of delight. "I know just where we are now," she cried. "There's the movie theater and Armored Force Headquarters, just as Mums described it. And now, I'll bet we turn left, then we turn right along the parade ground. . . . Oh, Terry!" She clutched his arm and pointed past the plain where some soldiers were drilling. "There's our house, in that row over there. I'm looking right at it."

"What's the number?"

"I don't know. Fourteen something-or-other, Fifth Avenue. But it's there." Penny's finger began moving and she counted, "One, two, three. . . . Oh, there it is! I see Tippy's bike out in front. That's our house, because Mums said the shrubbery has grown above the dining-room windows, and it has a sunroom on the end and oak trees and a weeping willow. And those are our rose drapes, and our car in the garage. And the good old piece of tin with 'Colonel David Parrish' printed on it is fastened to the iron railing beside the front steps. Terry, I'm *home!*"

Penny was out of the car before the driver could open the door for her. She stood feasting her eyes on the house before she turned back and tried to say quietly, "Come in, Terry, and have some breakfast with us. And we'd like to have you stay here instead of at the club if you'd care to. I know there's plenty of room."

"Thanks, Pen. I'll have to report in now and I know I'll have a room assigned to me, but I'd like to drop in tonight if I may."

"We'd love it." She wanted him to go. She wanted the soldier to leave her luggage on the lawn. But she had to follow the luggage up the walk, see it set neatly inside the hall while she held the door open, had to say, "Thank you again, and good-by," before she could close the thick white door and lean against it, listening to soft singing in the kitchen and the sound of bed-making upstairs.

She was home. Not as she had come many times before, from school or a friend's; but from a far, far place, a place that already had become as dim as a dream. She listened to the sounds about her for a few moments, the footsteps and clatter of dishes, then tip-toed to the stairway, cleared her throat and called upward:

"Whoo-hoo. I'm home. Your bad penny has turned up."

"Penny!" There was a glad cry from above and the sound of running feet. Mrs. Parrish whisked through the hall and around the stairwell, calling, "Oh, darling, darling!"

Her gay printed housecoat billowed out behind her, and when Penny met her halfway on the stairs their brown curls mingled.

"You haven't changed a bit," they both cried together.

Penny's mother had often been mistaken for an older sister. Her eyes were the same rich brown as Penny's, a little softer and steadier, but ready to fill with gay dancing lights; and her hair, worn shorter and brushed back from her face, had no gray in it. Penny's father often called them "the Parrish girls," and they in turn pointed out that he could see his own reflection in David's blue-eyed shining blondness. Even the lanky Bobby was an awkward caricature, with his sun-bleached hair in a crew-cut and his features not quite sure of the shape they would take. Only Tippy was different. Her eyes had become a golden-flecked mixture of both the blue and the brown and her curls were richer in red. And now Penny stopped hugging her mother to ask about her.

"Where's Tip?" she said.

"At school. And Daddy's been at the regiment lo, these many hours. He goes at the crack of dawn. And guess what?" They had started down the stairs but she stopped to exclaim, "Bobby will be home for the week-end!"

"Whoops!" Penny gave her mother another quick hug then whirled to hang perilously over the banister. "Trudy?" she shouted. "Trudy, my love, where are you?"

A door at the back of the hall flew open and, as a very small colored woman in a voluminous white apron looked out, Penny clattered down the stairs.

"Oh, Trudy, Trudy!" she cried, catching her around the waist and whirling her out into the hall, "I'm home! I'm home forever and a day—for three whole weeks!"

"Law, Miss Penny, honey." Most of Trudy's breath had been squeezed out, but she managed to grin and return the embrace. "Things'll be fine around here now, with all my children under one roof," she said, "jes' like when you was little."

"Only we're kinder to you now—we behave better."
Penny laughed up at her mother who was coming down the
stairs.

"But I reckon you still eat. I reckon you could still do
with a piece of chocolate chiffon pie." Trudy's eyes were
twinkling, and Penny clasped her hands over her heart and
breathed:

"Oh, could I! And I'll bet you have some hidden away.
Now you go straight out to the kitchen and find me a piece,
a *big* piece. And a pot of coffee, and some toast. I haven't
had any breakfast."

"Dear, dear." Trudy's loving face that had reflected the
moods of the Parrishes for more than twenty years, was a
pucker of resentment at the inconsiderate railroads. "You
should have sat right down in the station and eaten," she
scolded. "A few minutes more or less don't matter half so
much as your food, Miss Penny."

"I couldn't. I caught a ride out with Terry Hayes."

"With Terry?" For a second Marjorie Parrish was frightened as her mind flew to hasty war marriages and the unpre-
dictable things girls were rushing into now. Terry Hayes is
sweet, she thought desperately, though I'm sure he isn't the
one.... Penny was watching her expression and laughing.

"He's on some sort of inspection trip, lamb," she explained, "so don't worry. If you'll come into the living-
room-of-my-dreams I'll tell you all about it."

"Well, thank goodness."

Her mother followed her and curled up in one corner of
the divan while Penny, in a chintz chair with a small table
before her, consumed an amazing amount of pie and toast.

Up Goes the Curtain

"So you see, he's as crazy as ever," she ended, finishing the story of Terry and the last swallow of coffee at the same time. "And now about me. I got the part in the play."

"Of course, you did. I knew you would. Why, I told your father last night. . . ."

The telephone rang, and as she broke off to answer it, she said, "It's sure to be Carrol. She always calls at this time—and what shall I tell her?"

"Nothing." Penny was out of her chair and snatching up her coat in the hall. "Just tell her to stay at home, that you're coming over, or something. I want to surprise her."

She listened impatiently to her mother's voice that was as balmy as the weather outside, and when the receiver was back in its place asked, "How do I get there?"

"Go straight down the street and turn to the right. After a hundred yards or so you'll see a sign that says . . ."

"I know. Angel Alley." Penny chuckled as she threw open the door. " 'By. Tell Trudy to whip up a big lunch 'cause I'm still hungry."

She could scarcely keep from singing as she swung along the streets, reading nameplates on the houses and looking at forsythia bushes that were bursting with yellow, at spongy grass turning green, and spangled with the bright heads of crocuses.

I'm home, she thought happily, walking backward to see the flag, high on its pole against the bright blue of the sky, home in my dear army world that's peaceful and strong and sure, even in wartime.

And she loved even Angel Alley, which was a narrow street, lined with small houses that either had been hastily nailed together or transplanted whole or in sections, when the Government bought tracts of land for its great reservation. One, she was sure, was Carrol's.

It was little larger than a box car and, like all the others, was painted a doleful gray. But its shrubbery was carefully tended, and it had white lawn furniture under an oak tree from which a flagstone walk led to the barbecue pit David had built. Penny understood why David called it a shack and Carrol admired it, for it was a charming combination of both.

She skipped over the two steps that held up a dot of a portico, admiring the fine "Captain Parrish" on a black and white sign, and threw open the door. "Hey," she said, "it's me."

Carrol was sitting at her desk in the living room, and she looked around. She could see the whole house from where she sat, the bedroom, the kitchen, and the nook of a dining alcove; and when she saw Penny in the middle of it, she gave a leap that brought them together in the geographical center of things.

"You're still so darned beautiful," Penny said, after they had hugged and laughed and hugged again. "You ought to look like a hag, but you don't. Imagine you scouring and cooking and cleaning all this." She waved her arms and looked around the rooms that were as immaculate and beautiful as a model cottage, and Carrol sat down and laughed up at her.

"It's easy," she said. "I adore it."

"While I live in luxury with all your servants. David ought to be ashamed for us both."

Up Goes the Curtain

"David's my best butler." Carrol's eyes that were violet-blue, shone through their long dark lashes when she spoke of her young husband, and Penny thought for the hundredth time in her life that she had never seen anyone so lovely. Carrol's blond hair lay softly on the shoulders of her red wool dress, and sitting on the gold brocade divan with her slender hands clasped around her knees, she was even more beautiful than the painting of her mother which hung in the drawing-room of the Houghton's summer home at Gladstone.

"It's no wonder the dope's crazy about you," Penny said, laughing a little, "but the question your sister Penny wants answered is: Can *you* still bear him?"

"He's wonderful! He . . ."

"Don't tell me. I lived with him for eighteen tortured years of my life before you took him off the family's hands." Penny tossed her coat on a chair, dismissing David completely, then took three steps that put her in the kitchen doorway. "Look," she said, eyeing the secretive white front of the refrigerator, "do you have any cokes in this mousetrap?"

CHAPTER III

THE PARRISHES sat at dinner. Penny was close to her father where he loved her to be, and she had only to reach out a hand and touch David's olive drab sleeve.

There had been a moment of tense excitement at noon when the two men had come home and she had popped out from the hall coat closet and shouted, "Surprise, surprise!" Now she fitted in as one of the family, and it was as if she never had been away. She loved them all so much. And she looked around the table, letting her eyes linger on first one then another, until they encountered Tippy who was regarding her over a forkful of food.

"What's on your mind, Tip?" she asked.

A faint pink blush stole over Tippy's round cheeks, then she laid down her fork and spoke her thoughts as the Parrishes were accustomed to do. "I was just wondering," she said, "if I'd rather be exciting like you are when I grow up, or all shining and happy like David."

Laughter greeted her remark and her blush flared like a sunrise until David leaned an elbow on the table, wagged a finger at her, and said:

"Listen, Tippy. Don't let anyone kid you—you've got something there. Being a man, I can have my wife and a career, both. Perhaps Pen can, too. If she can't . . ."

"She will." Penny, in turn, rested her elbows on the table, and said soberly, "I know that being married and happy is the most beautiful thing in the world. When I'm here at home and see Mums and Dad every day I realize how—how wonderful it is. But I can't help it because something inside of me whips me along like a giant with a stick. I have to try expressing myself."

"Of course you do, Penny." Her father smiled at her and patted her hand. "Your mother and I know that. We wouldn't want you to sit around waiting for someone to marry."

"But she may never get anyone," Tippy remarked, virtuously resuming her meal and enjoying the sound waves she had stirred up. "I 'spect she'll be an old maid."

"Then she'll be a happy one." Carrol got up to help Trudy clear the table, and as the others pushed back their chairs, Penny stared dreamily at the jonquils in the centerpiece and said:

"We're a remarkable family. Here I am, almost famous, and we talk about me as if I weren't worth a whoop."

"You aren't yet, darling," her mother answered, reaching across her for a salt shaker. "You're just a little girl who is trying her wings."

"An' mighty floppy wings they is, at that." Trudy looked across the pile of plates she held and Penny jumped up from the table and laughed.

"I just love us!" she cried, laying the lace place mats one on top of another and enumerating with each one: "I love the way David's eyebrows bunch out when he frowns; and the odor of cleaning fluid that's always clinging to Tip; and the way you, Mums, put your glass in so exactly the same place after you drink from it; and Trudy's hands clasped under her apron. . . . Sometimes," she sighed, gathering up the rest of the mats and shoving them into a drawer, "I'm so filled with love I think I can't bear it."

"I know." Carrol set a chair straight and pulled Penny into the living room. "We are nice, but you're a little slap-happy tonight."

And she repeated that to David when they got home. She had turned on all the lamps, watching him while he took a cigarette from a silver box on the coffee table; and when he found his way to a deep chair, she sat on the wide uphol-stered arm.

"Penny's happy to be here," she said. And then she asked abruptly, "Do you suppose she could be upset because Terry was with another girl on the train?"

"Who? Marcia?" David reached out and pulled her into the chair with him. "Did Pen tell you about Marcia?"

"Of course, but where did you hear it?"

"From Terry. I saw him for half an hour this morning, and twenty-nine minutes of it was devoted to Marcia Mc-Main."

"Oh." Carrol drew back and looked at him. "Then that's an end of it for Penny," she said sadly. "I've always liked Terry."

David drew her head down to his shoulder, ground his cigarette into an ash tray, then laid his cheek against hers. "Listen, sweet," he said softly, "I'm going to have to see a lot of the fair Marcia for awhile, and I told Terry this morn-ing that there would be no show on unless you're in on it. He finally gave the okay because you're a mum little oyster. So. . . . You know what Terry's job is, don't you?"

"Why, yes. He's a G2."

"And what *is* G2, my new army wife?"

"I don't know." Carrol laughed and moved her cheek ever so little to feel David's scratching against it.

"Terry's in intelligence. And part of his job is to. . . ."

"David!" Carrol pushed both hands against his chest and sat up with a gasp. "Marcia's a spy," she whispered, staring at him. "She is, isn't she?"

But David only grinned at her. "I don't know," he said, shaking his head. "That's our job to find out."

"How?"

"By letting her think she's seeing some of our new stuff and then watching her. Terry thinks she's up to something, and wants me to play dumb and easy to get. Think I can do it?"

"Of course." Carrol sank back with a thrill of excitement. "Aren't you—and weren't you?" she teased.

"And could you be a bit jealous, just to make it look real?" David put both arms around her, held her close, and said softly, "You never have been, you know, Carrol. You've never doubted anything I ever did, or fussed or grouched."

"You haven't either." Carrol rested in the security of his arms knowing that this lamp-lighted room was a small perfect world within a large imperfect one. She almost forgot Terry and his problem until David said:

"Isn't it a crime, when there's such a beautiful part to be played, that Penny can't do it?"

"Oh, can't she help, David? She'd love it."

"She'd overplay the scene. Penny babbles like the well-known brook. And that's why poor old Terry had to suffer tortures on the train. I'll bet he suffers more before Pen gets through with him."

"Poor Terry, he will."

They sat in the chair, laughing a little at the innocent victims, tired, but too comfortable to move. Finally David yawned and said, "Marcia's coming out to the post tomorrow, to stay a few days at the Central Mess. I'll ask Terry to bring her to dinner if you think you can manage it, and I'll devote myself to her like a knight in shining armor. I'll be struck by a bolt of lightning and go around in a daze."

"Can Pen come, too?"

"Oh, I suppose so." David yawned again and pushed Carrol to her feet. "I'll dig up another man somewhere," he said grudgingly. "Now let's turn in and call it a day. Ask Mums to send Trudy over if you get stuck."

"I'll manage. I'll make the meal simple."

But however simple the menu looked, written on paper, she was up early to do her marketing, and was at the sink, her pink sweater and skirt covered by a shorter replica of Trudy's apron, when Penny appeared in the door.

"My word," Penny said, leaning against the wall and staring. "What's going on?"

"We're giving a party, so pitch in and help." Carrol took another apron from a drawer and tossed it across the room, but Penny only caught it and asked:

"Who's coming?"

"Why . . ." Carrol almost answered, "Terry and Marcia," but she stopped, inspected an apple for wormholes and explained casually, "David phoned that he had asked Terry

45

and another captain to dinner. Terry asked to bring some girl who'll be on the post, and I gather it's Marcia."

"Hm." Penny put on the apron and stood smoothing its starched folds. "I think I'll wear my new Kelly green crepe," she decided. "It has a peg-top drape that is *but* sophisticated. And maybe I'll do up my hair and put on the diamond earrings Gram left me." Her head tipped back as if pulled by the weight of piled-up curls and she took a swaying step toward the sink. "Perhaps I should have a long cigarette holder, although I never smoked in my life."

Carrol grinned at her over the head of lettuce she was washing, and Penny leaned against the drain board and answered with a flash of mirth. "I'm a nut," she laughed. "I couldn't be sophisticated if I tried."

"Neither one of us could."

"Well, you have a cool perfection that makes anyone who tries to sparkle synthetically look like a diamond bracelet out of the dime store."

"Thank you. Perhaps Marcia isn't out of the dime store."

"Oh, no?" Penny pushed Carrol over in order to pull a stool from under the sink, and when she was comfortably seated, folded her hands in her lap and said, "She's a gal who's on the up and up. I've seen her type before: smart and suave. And she didn't cook up a reason to follow Terry out here for nothing."

"Perhaps she's in love with him."

"Hunhuh, not Marcia." Penny leaned over and rested her crossed arms on her knees. "She's after something."

"Marriage, perhaps; girls often are. And now, how about peeling some spuds and putting them in cold water?"

Up Goes the Curtain

Carrol pushed the potato sack across the sink because she knew how Penny's imagination could work. It was like a road that went up hill and down, around breath-taking turns and through wild, unexplored country. It could tunnel through mountains or ford streams, for it always pursued its way to an end. Not always to the expected end, but to a terminus that satisfied it. Just now it seemed to be leading straight to the United States War Department, and Carrol jumped when Penny said thoughtfully:

"Something about Terry has been puzzling me. Something he said that I can't quite remember. I thought about it last night when I was thinking about him and Marcia. He acts so queer ... and he said. ..."

"Look, lamb, lend me a hand with the potatoes. Shall I brown them around the roast or mash them?" Carrol held out a knife, and Penny took it in absent-minded reverie, then sat staring at the potato she impaled on its point.

"He said ... something about. ... Oh, I know! He said he's a G2 at Fort Dix; and that's where they concentrate troops to go overseas. I wonder if Marcia knows that? I'll bet she. ..."

Carrol let a laugh ring out. It was a good laugh and she was proud of it. "Listen, idiot," she said. "I haven't seen Marcia, but Terry talked quite a bit about her to David. He seems to think she's rather special—and he isn't stupid, you know. Terry's a smart officer. You've said you don't want to marry him, so why spoil his romance? Please," she coaxed, "quit being silly and get to work."

"But he is stupid," Penny persisted, "about girls. And there are hundreds of secret agents around. Why, a girl I know caught a man taking pictures of the railroad tracks near Fort Arden; and on one of the posts an officer in our very own uniform hid in the shrubbery under a window to listen to a secret conference. It happens all the time. Terry's in a position to know things, and he talks too much. So I'm going to sleuth a little."

"Penny," Carrol dropped her work and all pretense, "it's just because you don't like the girl," she said desperately, hating the hurt she was inflicting on Penny's pride. "So don't be silly and make yourself look foolish and jealous to Terry. Marcia's probably just a nice girl who's coming to visit on the post."

"Have I ever been jealous of girls?" Penny's eyes came up, brown and clear, and, looking into them, Carrol had to shake her head.

"No," she sighed, "but you do get carried away by crazy ideas, Pen; you know that."

"This isn't a crazy idea—it's a hunch. And I'm going to step in and see what I can find out."

"And have everyone laughing at you."

"Oh, no." Penny cut a white path in the potato. "Oh, no," she said, leaning over to let the paring fall in the sink. "Little old Penny's a good actress. She can do a part off the stage as well as on."

"Well, I wish you'd do an easier one." Carrol tried to make light of the situation as she turned away. "Here I am, giving a party and you're wanting to spoil it by stalking around like Sherlock Holmes in a draped skirt. I shouldn't be surprised if you snatched away our forks, sprinkled powder on them, and took our fingerprints."

48

"Not yours, darling; just Marcia's." Penny giggled on her stool. "And no one but you need know what I'm doing."

"Oh, dear." There were only two things on Carrol's frantic mind. One was a wish to get to the telephone and David's comforting voice; and the other was the knowledge that she must handle Penny's uncanny suspicion alone. "Perhaps we'd better not have the party," she said, opening the refrigerator and staring into its well-filled interior. "It's such an awful lot of work."

"I'll be good. I'll help." Penny began briskly on her potato again, but Carrol only closed the solid white door and leaned against it. She wanted to put up an obstacle that would start Penny's mind on a detour, so she announced:

"I didn't mention it before, but David and I have put in our order for a very special baby."

"You *have?*" Penny's eyes were wide with joy and surprise. "Well, my goodness." Down into the sink went her work again as she jumped off her stool. "What will you do with it if David goes overseas?" she asked.

"Love him and take care of him until David comes home. That's why we want him—so I won't be so lonely."

"Well, well!" Penny crossed the small kitchen and put her arms around Carrol. "I think it's thrilling," she said, grinning and patting Carrol's back. "I'll help you with him. I'll even roll his pram in the park. When I'm not at the theater I'll feed him and dress him. . . ."

"Would you mind helping with the dinner instead?" Carrol was laughing because Penny was caring for a baby they didn't yet have.

But back at their work she sighed. Penny's words were of bonnets and pink silk coats and toys, but where, Carrol wondered, was her run-away mind?

CHAPTER IV

THE PARTY had moved along nicely and Terry was devoting himself to Penny. He had pulled a small chair close to hers and was leaning forward, his demitasse held between his knees, the black coffee cooling while he listened to her in a way that should have been gratifying but wasn't, because Penny was watching David on the divan with Marcia. There was no doubt that David was enjoying Marcia and that he was unaware of Carrol's exit to the kitchen. It raised Penny's spirits a little to watch the other guest follow her, a presentable and sleekly dark young captain in the air force, and to hear their laughter as they tenderly wrapped the remains of the roast in waxed paper. But, like a fluffy parasol that is no good in the rain, her spirits drooped again when Carrol returned with the silver coffee pot and David held out his cup without so much as looking at her.

Never before had he failed to turn from whatever he was doing, or from anyone with whom he was talking. He could batter his way across a crowded dance floor to reach her, could let the family sit with unfinished sentences when she entered a room, could listen politely to a high-ranking officer, while he reached out to draw her close to him. Now he reached out, but only for more coffee, and he did it as if Trudy were pouring it for him.

Penny's eyes flashed and she got up and crossed the room.

Up Goes the Curtain

"I'll pour," she said, forcefully taking the pot and setting it beside the silver cream pitcher and sugar bowl on the coffee table. "Move over, David, and let me in here."

She squeezed across him and sat down in the exact center of the divan where she began the delicate business of filling Marcia's cup and successfully blocking her off from the rest of the room. And as she poured the dark liquid she stilled a desire to let it dribble like a jet necklace across Marcia's beige-colored lap.

But Marcia smiled at her and relinquished David without so much as a sad sweep of her eyes; so Penny set the coffee pot down again and was relieved to find that David had at last recognized his wife. She offered herself a mental handshake of congratulations, but her triumph was short-lived for she had a busy evening. David and Marcia were always discovering each other. They met over an album of records; they lighted cigarettes at the same moment, sharing the match; they even resorted to card tricks. And only once did Carrol send a worried little frown along the length of the room.

Penny saw it go, like a frightened S. O. S. that had got off the beam and so never reached its destination, and she knew it was Marcia who bent her head carelessly toward David and intercepted it. So she said to Terry, close at her side again, "Look here, my good man, you brought this boneless, toneless wonder into our midst—she belongs to you, so how about removing her? She doesn't fit in."

"Maybe not, but she's something to look at."

"So's an oil painting—of fish."

Up Goes the Curtain

Terry laughed and looked down, teasing her. "What're you so hot and bothered about?" he asked. "It's a time for rejoicing. David takes over and you have me."

"I don't want you."

"Not even if you could have me, complete with wedding ring and all my worldly goods?"

"Not even then." Penny shook her head emphatically. "You spend all your worldly goods, which, I might add, consist of a very nice paycheck each month, on girls like...." She stopped, motioned with her head to the couple dancing before the radio, and Terry grinned and finished her sentence for her.

"On girls like you and Marcia," he said.

"Terry Hayes!" Penny's eyes flashed sparks and she drew herself up very straight. "I am not anything like Marcia."

"Oh, come now, Pen. I was only kidding." He tried to rest an elbow on the mantel which was too low and flimsy, so had to content himself with leaning against the wall beside it. "Marcia's really a nice girl," he pointed out, "and you'd like her if you'd give yourself a chance."

"Marcia's a nice girl," she mimicked, envying people in stories who "snorted" their remarks. "You say so, Carrol says so, and it's most apparent that David *thinks* so. Only I stand alone with my opinion. Well," she sighed, "*I* don't think so."

"Because David seems to like her?"

Carrol crossed the room to them before she could answer, and swinging hands with her, Penny said to Terry, "You may have that reason if you like; it's as good as any." Then, with a toss of her head, she went off to devote herself to Captain Forsythe who was idly turning the pages of a magazine. This brought her quite close to David and she heard him say:

"Why don't you have Terry bring you out to the division club sometime? I'll take you to lunch and show you around."

Marcia's reply was lost to her, even though she leaned forward as if adjusting her sandal; and she would have been surprised and thrown completely off balance had she heard it, for Marcia answered:

"Thanks, but I'm no good at sight-seeing. My mother dragged me through all the cathedrals in Europe one summer and it marked me for life, I suppose. I'm really very lazy."

They stopped dancing, and David turned off the record. As he lifted the needle arm he looked down at her and smiled. "I don't think so," he said. "This may be a rather stupid comparison, but I think you're like a carefully banked fire. It smolders quietly in the grate, and then in the dead of night, it bursts into flame and lights up a dark, empty room with startling clarity." He ended the sentence with an ardent look and thought to himself, wow, I hope I can remember to tell that one to Carrol; and was so busy memorizing it that he started when Marcia answered:

"Captain, you are much too discerning."

"Just call me David."

"David, then."

"And you'll come to lunch?"

"No." Marcia shook her smooth head and regarded him

seriously. "I like you very much ... David," she said. "Very much. But you're married, you know."

"Oh." David ran his hand through his hair, tousling the short curls a little and looking surprised. "Carrol wouldn't care," he declared. "Why, she...."

They both turned to look at Carrol who was laughing with Terry, but Marcia shook her head again. "I may smolder, David," she said with a smile, "but I don't burn innocent victims."

David hoped his sigh of relief was not too audible. He felt happy for the first time that evening and with his release so plainly delivered, grinned in good companionship. "Let's dance again," he said, starting the record wherever the needle happened to fall. "You're a beautiful dancer."

Penny heard the last four words, as did everyone else in the room, and clapped the magazine shut with the pop of a cap pistol. "It's time to go home," she announced, getting up from the divan and marching into the bedroom for her hat and coat. When she came back, twisting her hat between her fingers, she stood at the door and refused to look at David while she said good night. "Nice party, Carrol," she mumbled. "See you tomorrow."

"Will you be over in the morning?" Carrol leaned against the open door longing to give Penny's stiff little shoulder a hug, and trying not to laugh at the misery of David.

"Penny," David offered uncomfortably, grasping the first remark that leaped into his mind, "do you want me to walk home with you?"

"Well, for goodness' sake!" Penny flung up her head and stared at him coldly. "How could you leave your guest -*s?*"

she said, with such a sibilant plural that Captain Forsythe, also with his cap in his hand, laughed and thought her amusing.

"I'm taking her home, Dave," he announced, grinning, opening the screen door and giving her a gentle start. "We may drive out to the Hunt Club though, for a dance or two. Why don't you and Carrol come later?"

"We might." David watched Penny sweep down the steps, and sighed. "Darn the war," he muttered, closing the door and, since his back was turned to the room, dropping a kiss on Carrol's nose. "Pen and I never have fought, so I guess you'd better tell her before she upsets the whole family."

"No." Carrol shook her head. "This is *war*, David," she whispered, "and it's none of Penny's business, or mine, or the family's."

"But if Marcia's okay—and it looks as if she is. . . ."

"We don't know. You're doing a job. And that's all you can do, darling." She closed the door and led him back to his guests, smiling and suggesting the Hunt Club.

"Can't," Terry answered regretfully. "Tomorrow's another work day. I have to look over a half-track that David's company's testing. Come on, Marcia."

"Oh, *Terry*." Marcia threw him a glance of longing but he shook his head.

"See you on the tank course at ten, Dave," he said. "We'll have a look at that new gun turret; it ought to be good."

David nodded, but when they were gone, he said thoughtfully to Carrol, "Terry's nuts."

"Why?"

Up Goes the Curtain

"Because we *have* a new type of turret."

Carrol stopped with the ash trays she was carrying to the kitchen. "Perhaps he knows that if Marcia is smart, she knows it, too," she answered. "If she's really looking for something, that is."

But David shook his head. "I don't really think she's looking. But it isn't good to talk about stuff like that. I don't mention it here at home."

"For fear I'd say something?"

"For fear *anyone* would say something. Terry's taking a chance."

They talked it over in short worried sentences while they put their small house in order, and only a few blocks away two other people were worrying over the same problem. Penny tossed restlessly in her bed, and under a desk lamp in his small bachelor's cubicle, Terry scowled at a blank sheet of paper. An hour passed while he sat, tapping his pen on a scarred green blotter. At last and with a sigh, he pulled the paper toward him, scrawled the date and his commanding officer's name, then the few words, "Nothing at all to report, sir."

Marcia let herself into her pine-paneled room in the Central Mess, closed her door, and hummed while she undressed and carefully cold creamed her face.

She slipped into a gown and green satin negligee, picked up a book from the dresser, then laid it down to open her evening purse and take out a letter. The light in the little room was poor, so she moved a lamp from one side of the dresser to the other, and sat down on the foot of the bed to read.

Up Goes the Curtain

The thick paper crackled as she unfolded it, and she smiled at the first few paragraphs, then frowned in concentration at the words: "I have just learned that Carl Sommers is stationed at Knox. I know that a cousin isn't particularly interesting to run around with, especially when he's only a private, first-class, but Aunt Mattie wants you to look up Carl. The boy has plenty of money and can show you around. She says he gets lonely hanging around the Service Club Number 1, so you might drop over there and surprise him. Have a good time, honey, but don't stay away too long."

The letter was signed, 'Dad"; and she read it through twice before she shrugged, tore it into little pieces, and tossed it into the waste paper basket. Then she yawned, turned out her inadequate light, slid into bed and into a dreamless sleep.

CHAPTER V

Penny arrived at Carrol's so early the next morning that Carrol, on the divan, lowered her newspaper, put down the coffee cup she was lifting to her mouth, and remarked slyly, "Your family must be enjoying your visit."

"Pooh." Penny shed her tan plaid topcoat by the simple means of giving it a yank, shrugging out of it, and letting it fall behind her on a chair. "Bobby gets home tonight and Mums is running in circles and trying to find enough food to last him over the week-end. She won't even miss me. Let's get going."

"Get going? No, thanks." Carrol reached for her cup again and said over its rim, "I've been going since six-thirty, pet. David went out like a fire truck, and I've done my homework, and now I'm catching my breath. There's more coffee on the stove if you want it."

"My goodness." Penny scoffed at anyone who needed more than a few hours' rest, then went off to the kitchen with a sigh. "There's so much to do," she called back over the rattle of china, "and I thought we'd go out to the club for lunch."

"Why?"

"It's nice out there, and we have to go somewhere. We can't just *sit* all the time." She came back carrying a plate with a cup on it and a large slice of bread and butter and jam, and went on talking while she pulled a small table from its nest of three and set it in front of a chair. "Three weeks go by in a flash," she explained, "and I have a lot to do."

"Such as. . . ."

"Lunching, dining, dancing, and . . ."

"And pursuing Marcia."

"Huh?" Penny paused with the slice of bread halfway to her mouth and Carrol laughed.

"You're incurable," she said. "I've known you for over five years and there's never been a time when you weren't going at problems as if they were cross word puzzles."

"Yes, and sometimes I finish 'em." Penny grinned too, and asked complacently, "Are we going?"

"Oh, I suppose so, though I have to be at Red Cross at two."

"David isn't coming home at noon, is he?"

"No."

"Then we'll drive out early. He might pop into the club."

She was very busy with her second breakfast and Carrol opened her mouth to speak, then closed it again, and sat watching her. It was of no use to tell Penny that David had said he would be on the tank proving ground all day, for she wouldn't believe it; so she pulled a pillow higher and leaned back, loving David, and seeing him with a group of officers on the muddy track, watching a tank as it slid down a slippery bank and plowed its way out of the ditch; checking the guns, the visibility, the power of attack. David had told her a great deal about his work and she was lost in her own interesting thoughts when Penny asked:

"Did you two have a fight last night?"

"Mercy, no!" Carrol folded the newspaper and got up to lay it on the table beside David's special chair, and said over her shoulder, "We've never had a fight in our life, and you know it. I can't imagine anyone ever wanting to fight with David."

"Well, I can." Penny, too, began the business of straightening up. Later in the morning, however, when they were driving toward the small rustic club that was a recreation center for the officers of the division, she promised herself silently, "If he comes into the dining room with that camouflaged stick of dynamite, I'm going to rend him limb from limb!"

But she had no cause to worry, for David was as absent in the circle of diners as is the center in a doughnut. They had such a quietly expensive luncheon, that when Carrol pecked at an uninteresting salad she thought of the good cold lamb in her refrigerator. And when Penny dropped her off at the low brick building that housed the Red Cross and suggested, "Let's do it again tomorrow," she shook her head.

"The budget won't take it," she said. "I'll give you a sandwich at home. And, by the way, David and I'll be over to dinner tonight."

"Okay."

Penny slipped the car into gear and wondered what she would do with the rest of her afternoon. There was on the seat a library book that her mother wanted exchanged, so she turned the car and paused at the corner to wonder where the library might be. A passing soldier pointed vaguely toward a road that wandered off into a lane of trees, and as she pursued it slowly, she noticed a girl walking ahead of her. Penny shoved down on the brake so suddenly that the car rocked on its springs like a cradle. She sat watching the girl turn into a white Colonial building which bore a sign above its tall pillars SERVICE CLUB NO. I.

"Well," Penny said to herself, "that's Miss Marcia or I'll eat my fur hat. Now *what* is she doing in there?"

She sat quite still in the car for some minutes, wondering how she could get into the club, wishing she were a WAC, or a Gray Lady, or even a mouse. A detective always manages to impersonate someone else in a crisis, but without a good disguise Penny knew she would have to enter as Penny, who, with no business on hand, would stand out like the Statue of Liberty.

"To be, but not to be," she quoted inaccurately. "That is the question. Whether it is safer for my mind to suffer the pangs and tortures of outrageous curiosity, or to take up arms against them, and by so doing...." Without waiting to finish her liberties with Shakespeare she drove into a parking lot across from the enlisted men's club and climbed out of the car.

She reconnoitered a little before entering the building, by the simple method of cupping her hands against the screen door and peering into a dim hall that had a large club room beyond it and offices on each side. There were wide-open double doors at the end of the hall and she whisked the few feet to them, closed one door a little, and stood in its shadow with her hand high on its edge so that the sleeve of her coat shielded her face. This gave her an excellent view of the big room which had a polished floor for dancing and comfortable chairs and divans around its sides, and even let her peek into a soda fountain and restaurant on her left. A hostess was seated at a table in a far corner of the room, and with her was

Marcia. They were talking earnestly and Penny wondered what there was about Marcia that made her look so different. She seemed younger, and her eyes weren't long gray slits; they were wide open and free of mascara, and her hair hung softly, almost to her shoulders. Looking at her, one would notice that Marcia was pretty—and that was all. Even her suit was the college girl type.

She and the hostess were enjoying their chat, but after a few moments Marcia got up and walked across the dance floor to the soda fountain where she sat at a table and toyed with a chocolate sundae that made Penny envious. Two girls came in the front door with a clatter and Penny stepped out from her hiding place and began a hurried fumbling in her purse. One of the girls stopped to watch her, and with a murmured, "Oh, I've left my keys in the car," Penny dashed out and down the steps.

Now she was outside again, with nothing accomplished, and she walked slowly on to the car, wondering what to do next. There was no point in going back if Marcia were only planning to eat, so she slid onto the seat, reached for her mother's book, and decided to herself, "I'll trail her, or tail her, or whatever it is the cops do."

She read for some time, assiduously, but without knowing what the book was about, while she held her place with her finger in order to look up at half-minute intervals. The sun got down into the bare branches of the trees, and her legs were tired from being crossed so long. Soldiers began filtering into the club, and since Marcia stayed inside with them, Penny decided she would have to take another look.

She got stiffly out of the car, repeated her approach and

scuttle through the hall, and when she clung to her protecting door, was rewarded by the sight of Marcia sitting on a divan with a round-faced, carroty-headed soldier. He was the proud recipient of all her schoolgirl attention, which Penny thought a waste as there was nothing about him to warrant it.

She was watching Marcia study a photograph he had taken from his wallet, when the two girls appeared again, coming toward her like busy genii, and she was forced to disappear once more. Back in the car, she wondered how she had ever considered it comfortable transportation on a long trip. "I could have gone from here almost to Indianapolis," she computed, looking at her watch. "What a wasted afternoon. But maybe not."

At that moment Marcia appeared in the doorway, alone, and with a hasty crash of the starter, Penny whisked out of the parking place and let her have a back view of the car. Marcia came down the steps, took the road that led to the Central Mess, and when she was safely on well-traveled ground where a car might be coming from anywhere, Penny trundled up beside her and stopped.

"Want a lift?" she called.

"Thanks."

Marcia got in and Penny ostentatiously pushed her book forward on the seat, letting it speak for itself of her errand. "I didn't recognize you at first," she said.

"I was taking a walk. It's so lovely out and I'm so bored until Terry comes in. I didn't bother with make-up."

"No one does, around here." Penny turned her head for a long look and hoped she could do as well without "bother"

64

for her ingénue Drucilla on opening night. "Did you walk far?" she asked.

"Just to the Service Club. My father wanted me to look up a cousin and I thought I might as well do it and get it over."

She was so frank that Penny forgot to stop at the Central Mess. It was the longest speech Marcia had ever made to her, and when she added, "Wait, here's where I'm staying," Penny pulled in to the curb and asked eagerly:

"Did you find him?"

But Marcia was getting out of the car. "Thanks awfully for the lift," she said. "Shall we see you tonight?"

"I don't know. Jimmy Forsythe said something about the movies."

Penny resented Marcia's "we." It linked Terry to her, and perhaps David. She felt cross about her afternoon, the waiting, with Marcia offering information of her own volition, and she wished she dared repeat her question about the cousin. Her emotions flooded over her, and then, like a river that has suddenly decided to flow up-hill, they backwashed, leaving her ashamed of her doubt and spying. Marcia looked like such a nice girl, standing on the curb, a nice girl who has a misguided notion that it's smart to be sophisticated. So she leaned out and said, "Let's get Carrol and David, and all go together."

"All right, and thanks again." Marcia started up the brick walk to the club and, as Penny drove off, sent back a wave of her hand.

I guess Carrol's right, Penny thought, passing the empty flagpole and wishing she had come home in time to stand on the lawn and watch retreat. And perhaps I only imagined the sappy way David was acting. I've never seen him in his own home before and that may be just his goofy way of being a host.

She drove into the garage and opened the door that led both to the basement and the kitchen. Trudy was at the sink and, when Penny came up the few steps, turned to look at her.

"So you thought you'd come home," she said, holding out a scraped carrot before Penny could reach into the pan. "Seems like you might as well've stayed in New York."

"Umhum." Penny leaned against the sink and looked down at the carrot. "Trudy," she asked, "do you think I've grown up?"

"Law, Miss Penny, honey." Trudy wrinkled her brow and shook her head. "I cain't tell you, cause I don't ever see you."

"I know, but. . . . Look, Trudy. Do you think I could keep on making so many mistakes and being wrong about things? Things I feel? You used to say I never knew what I was trying to do."

"Does you now?"

"I think so. I decide things and I think I'm right . . . and then. . . ."

"Then you's improvin'!"

"And you think I ought to go on—sticking to what I've decided?"

"I don't say that, Miss Penny." Trudy took her pan of carrots to the stove and turned on the gas. "I jes' say, honey, that fo' you to be seein' two sides to a thing is improvement."

She chuckled comfortably and Penny took a bite from her carrot. "An' it's like this, too," she continued, drying her hands on a paper towel, "you gets yo' eyes so set on a goal that you can walk right through a stone wall to reach it. That's why you'll succeed."

"I'm not thinking of my career. I'm thinking that perhaps I've been unfair to someone—or perhaps I haven't. I had a hunch and I've been blindly following it. I've been so sure I was right."

"Don't ever be sure about folks. Jes' study 'em and kind of put yo'self in their place."

"I did that this afternoon. But people can fool you, you know."

"Yes'm, they can. But if they's honest, they ain't tryin' to. An' if they isn't honest they cain't do it f' long. That's all you have to know, Miss Penny."

"Thank you, Trudy, dear. I'll be open-minded—but watchful."

She gave Trudy's shoulder a pat and went through the hall and into the living room where her mother and father were sitting. "Hi, my darlings," she said, blowing them kisses. "Your daughter has returned to the fold; and I hope, Mums, that you will let your mind dwell upon your happy week-end with your son when I tell you that she forgot to exchange your library book."

CHAPTER VI

Young Bobby Parrish arrived just after dinner and was received into the family's arm like a long-legged colt that couldn't stand still long enough to be fondled. He galloped upstairs and down, with frequent foraging trips to the kitchen, and was followed by his faithful satellite, Tippy. The gap between their ages had widened and at fourteen, as a man of experience and a power on the athletic field, if not in the academic world, her third-grade innocence irked him.

"Listen, punk," he said, tired of pushing her curls out of the treasures he was displaying in his room, "that's Fatso's baseball mitt and you're smearing chocolate on it—and let Beany's wrist watch alone."

"Didn't you bring home any of your own things?" his mother asked, lifting an undershirt from the bed and examining the laundry mark.

"Sure. But we kind of like to trade around. Chink took my bathrobe and traded my slippers to Skinny for. . . ."

"Does anyone call you by your right name?" she interrupted. "By any chance would *anyone* call you Robert?"

"Hunhuh. I'm Legs. 'Cause I can run so fast," he added proudly, making a lunge that scattered his pile of soiled laundry. "Let my stuff alone, Tip."

The Parrishes enjoyed him for an evening; they gazed upon him with devotion, and if they sometimes winked at one another in irreverence and even amusement, he was blithely unaware that there were other worlds more important than his own. By morning he fitted in as Penny had done, and people passing by on the sidewalk, might have noticed that the long brick house had a smiling, complacent, look. Its shades were half-drawn like sleepy, contented eyes relaxed from watching, satisfied, at last, that a family was complete behind them.

The front door opened and closed proudly many times, and when it let Carrol out at five o'clock it stayed a little ajar because she forgot to close it. She was running across the lawn by the time the screen door banged, and as she ran she scanned all the cars that were carrying officers home from work, hoping one would be bringing David. But her convertible stood in its own graveled drive and she threw it only a glance as she sped by, flying over the steps like a Winged Victory.

"David!" she cried, gasping for breath and looking at him in the living room, at ease without his blouse and with a cold drink beside him, one long leg draped over the arm of his chair, the other on an ottoman. "Something awful has happened. Penny has invited Marcia to visit her!"

"*What?*" David sat up and scrubbed at the lemonade that spattered his tie. "Ye gods, *why?*"

"I don't know. She only said she thought she's been unfair to Marcia and that the Central Mess won't keep anyone but a few days, so tonight's her last night . . . and since she's come so far to be with Terry. . . ."

"I don't believe her." David set his glass on the table beside him without looking at it and Carrol crossed the room to rub out the wet ring it made. "Penny's nuts," he said.

"I don't think so." Carrol scrubbed at the mahogany surface of the table without really seeing it, then absent-mindedly set the glass on it again and stood watching the trickles of water run down. "I—I've been keeping something from you," she began, facing him squarely, then stooping to push his foot off the ottoman and sitting down. "I did it because I didn't want to worry you, but I guess I can't go on with it. Penny suspected Marcia of being a spy, right from the first."

"Good grief!"

"I tried to talk her out of it but she wouldn't believe me. Then she got mad when you made a fuss over Marcia, and has been dragging me out to the club...."

"Thank goodness, she didn't see me take her to lunch today!"

"Oh, did you, David? What did she do?"

"Not a darn thing."

Carrol was leaning forward and now she crossed her arms on his knee. "Did she flirt with you?" she asked.

"Nope." David was so matter-of-fact in his statement that Carrol laughed. "I ran into her and she said Terry had stood her up—he'd told me he was going to—so I asked her to go to chow with me. She acted just like anyone else around here," he went on, "and wouldn't even talk war." He reached across Carrol's head for his lemonade, offered her a sip, and said thoughtfully, "I think Terry's barking up the wrong tree, and I wish Pen would keep her nose out."

"She won't, though. And if she ever finds out that the F.B.I. put Marcia on Terry's list...."

"Don't let her." David finished his drink in a gulp and leaned back with a tired frown between his eyes. "We aren't going over home to dinner tonight, are we?" he asked. "I've got a meeting at eight, and I'd like us to whip up a quiet meal for two if we can."

"We can." Carrol jumped up from the ottoman and started toward the kitchen but before she reached the dining room arch David's arm was around her.

"I'll peel," he said.

They laughed a great deal over their dinner, forgetting Marcia and the war, but when David had gone to his meeting, Carrol telephoned the Parrishes and asked for Penny.

"She's gone to the movies," Bobby informed her, in a voice that might have been two people talking, and one which included both his past and his future. "She went by herself and said if you and David called up to tell you to come on over."

Carrol explained about David's meeting, and asked, "What's the name of the picture?"

"Don't know, but it's swell. Gangsters an' crooks an' spies. Wow! I went this afternoon."

"Oh." Carrol had had quite enough of mysteries and, since Bobby proceeded to explain the picture to her with gestures that produced the sound effects of a vase crashing to the floor and his mother's scream, she laughed and hung up the telephone. She was sure Penny would stop by when the movie was over, so she picked up a book and began to read.

But Penny, sitting alone in the movie, already had become bored with the racket and gunfire on the screen and was debating within herself whether to suffer it out or to leave. The house was only half-filled, and letting her attention wander while she pulled her coat around her shoulders, she discovered Marcia sitting a few rows in front of her. Marcia was alone, too. Several seats on either side of her were vacant. And then Penny stared, slid out of her coat, and sat quite still. Marcia's row held the red-haired soldier! He was lounging in his chair between two other enlisted men and seemed quite unaware that his cousin was so near him.

With a thrill of excitement, Penny sat, tense and watching. Marcia was restless. Now and then she rubbed her forehead as if the noisy picture made her head ache, and after a few minutes she put on her hat. Penny, too, began getting ready to leave, but as Marcia rose from her seat she ducked behind the protecting screen of a large woman and her equally fat escort. Through a peephole she watched Marcia ease past the three soldiers. Marcia did it quietly, without looking away from the screen, and Penny was preparing to crawl across the long line that blocked her own exit, when she saw the red-haired soldier stoop, straighten, and say, "Oh, Miss, you dropped your glove."

Marcia was standing in the aisle. The soldier held out a black glove, and with a grateful smile that held no recognition, she reached out to him. Her trim head nodded her thanks, and then she tucked the glove into her pocket and went on. Penny began climbing over people's knees and treading on their feet. In a few seconds she, too, was in the aisle and was hurrying after Marcia who had disappeared down the stairs that led to the lobby. She lunged at the steps preparing to take them two at a time, when a familiar croak called, "Hey, Pen!" and there, blocking her progress, was Bobby.

"Oh, dear me," she cried, trying to push past him, "what are *you* doing here?"

73

"I came to find you and get some wampum. Mums and Dad went out, and the gang wants to. . . ."

"Oh, here!" Penny zipped open her purse and thrust a bill at him. "And don't tag after me."

"Why not? Can't you drive us. . . ?"

"No!" Penny was running down the stairs, grateful that only Bobby's surprised whistle followed her, although the whistle made her wonder if she had given him a five dollar bill instead of a one.

Marcia was just rounding a corner of the building when she came out, so Penny whisked around the other side and past her parked car. She tried to run without wasting breath so that, when Marcia crossed the graveled space behind the theater and walked toward a vacant lot which had a winding path across it to the Central Mess, Penny was strolling away from the cars and swinging the chain that held her ignition key.

"Hi," she called, "is the picture over?"

"No, but it made my head ache." Marcia showed no surprise at being confronted there, and Penny stood before her dangling her key.

"Wasn't it good?"

"I didn't care for it, but you might if you like gangsters. Everyone else seemed to get a bang out of it."

"I don't think I'll try it." Penny made a sudden decision and watched Marcia, waiting for any flicker of surprise or knowledge that the theater had held them both, but Marcia only said casually:

"Then how about walking home with me? Terry went to a meeting but we might have a soda until he comes."

"Okay, only I have a car. It's right over here."

They walked across the gravel together and Penny's fingers longed to reach inside Marcia's pocket and extract the glove that was rolled up inside it. A strange prescience told her there would be a piece of paper inside that glove, and she had no intention of losing Marcia until she had made a try for it.

"It could be a love letter," she argued with herself, standing close beside Marcia while she got into the car, and keeping an eye on her through the windshield when she had to walk around the hood and climb in beside her. "Perhaps I'm wrong and she's only two-timing Terry, but this is my country and I don't like the way she acts. Even Trudy says to be watchful."

Thus, having spread a thick paste of suspicion on her conscience and slapped it between two thick slices of patriotism, she proceeded to bite into the sandwich with relish. Marcia's coat was open, with its pocket resting on the seat between them, and Penny took her purse from her lap and laid it beside her, quite near enough to feel the tip of a glove that protruded. But Marcia pulled her coat politely away and leaned back in her corner. They talked casually, and when Penny pulled up before the Central Mess she was still without a plan for committing theft. Two-thirds of a gangster film had failed to help her because it was not a question of hitting Marcia over the head with a wrench, and then robbing her. It was a question of subtlety. And of all the qualities that had been crowded into the happy baby who had been presented to the Parrishes some nineteen years ago, subtlety was one quality too many for the tiny head to hold;

so it had been left out and given to someone else ... probably to Marcia.

For Marcia led the way into the club, sat on a stool before the soda fountain; and if she were at all worried about the contents of her pocket or the fact that Penny always maneuvered to be on her left, her white forehead remained smooth, and her eyes, behind their hedge of lashes, veiled and enigmatic. Twice Penny almost gave up and went home, but her stubbornness that had crowded out the subtlety held her on her stool until Terry came in and leaned over her shoulder.

"Hello," she said, watching Marcia's face light up with what she considered a false glow. "What was the meeting about?"

"Nothing much. Just a waste of time."

He stood between the two girls, and, looking into the mirror behind the counter, his eyes anxiously searched Penny's face. Without meaning to, he laid a hand on her shoulder and she looked up from her soda and drew away.

"Major Hayes," she drawled in mock embarrassment, "pul*ease!*"

"Sorry. I was only steadying myself." Terry smiled at Marcia and added, "Cute child, isn't she?"

"Very. Shall we go in the lounge and sit?"

"Suits me." Terry paid for the drinks while Penny followed Marcia like a faithful aide-de-camp.

The lounge was a large room filled with inviting furniture, and when Marcia chose a divan in a corner, Penny skirted an obviously comfortable chair for a place beside her. She sat with her hand resting on a cushion, the middle finger so near the protruding tip of glove, that when Marcia turned to watch Terry's approach Penny turned too, and with a twitch the glove came out.

Something crackled inside it. To Penny, it crackled so loudly it sounded like a rifle shot, and she held her breath while Marcia went on smiling upward. Then, inch by inch, with the barest motion of her fingers, she wiggled the glove down between the cushions. After that, it was comparatively easy to move over for Terry and sit on the crack.

But Penny could have been no more nervous had she been sitting on a bomb. The minutes dragged by into a half-hour, into an hour, with no one making a move to leave. Twice she shifted her position and pretended to smooth her skirts under her while each time she dug the glove from its groove and tried to roll it into a ball. And at last, with a desperate effort, she leaned back, put both hands under her, and gave herself a shove. "I have to go," she announced, springing upright and jamming both hands into her pockets. "I'm sleepy."

She gave a convincing yawn, casually covering her mouth with her left hand, and hoping thereby to project a sleight of hand performance that would focus two pairs of eyes on the wrong spot while she settled the glove firmly in its new hiding place. Then she ostentatiously adjusted her coat with both hands and gave an inward sigh of relief just as Terry said:

"Drive me home, will you, Pen?"

"All right."

Marcia was getting up, too, and Penny's heart almost stopped beating when Marcia said, "Stay awhile, Terry," and then slid her hand into her pocket.

Up Goes the Curtain

"I can't wait any longer," Penny interrupted, "really, I can't. It's so late . . . and Mums . . . you stay, though." She was going pell-mell across the floor without waiting to see what happened. Her one thought was to get away; but from the safe distance of half across the room she forced herself to turn and call, "I'll pick you up in the morning, Marcia, around eleven."

But Marcia and Terry were lifting the cushions of the divan and searching the floor.

"Marcia's lost her glove," Terry called, and she had to go back.

Oh, my goodness, she thought frantically, what if she accuses me of theft and they search me! She mumbled something and ran into the soda fountain, ostensibly to look under the stools but in reality to still her panic. Marcia can't raise a fuss about me stealing just one glove, she reasoned, stooping among the feet and litter on the floor and almost sobbing in her distress. If I say I found it. . . . Without stopping to reason further she pulled the black ball from her pocket, hastily extracted the note, then shoved the glove under her foot and gave it a swipe across the floor for good measure.

"Found!" she called triumphantly, holding it aloft as Marcia and Terry came in. "It's a mess but it'll clean."

"Thanks, so much. It's pre-war suede and I'd hate to lose it."

Marcia took the glove and, although she only smoothed it, Penny could see her fingers feeling for a bit of paper and her eyes making a sweep of the floor around her. "Now I *have* to leave," Penny said. "Coming, Terry?"

"I think I'll stay a few minutes."

"You'd better go." Marcia was quick to forestall him. "I'm tired."

"But you said . . ."

"I've changed my mind."

She looked so vexed and snapped out the words so rapidly that Penny muttered, "Good-by," and shot out of the door before Terry could make a decision. "Oh, me," she kept telling herself, clutching the note and running toward her car, "I'm a thief. I'm horrible, and ashamed—and yet I'm kind of proud of myself. Oh, dear!"

It was hard not to break the fifteen-mile speed limit and to wait for stop lights, but when finally she turned off her motor in the garage she tip-toed through the darkened house and was halfway up the stairs when a board creaked and her mother called:

"Is that you, Pen?"

"Umhum."

"Dad and I just came to bed so don't you want to come in and talk for a bit?"

"Not—not just now." Penny tore up the remaining steps and into her room. "I'm kind of sleepy," she explained inadequately, wishing she could stop shaking.

Even the door knob chattered as she closed the door, and when she turned on a lamp she failed for the first time in years to admire the rose and white beauty around her. The flowered chintz chaise longue with its heaps of pillows had always been a haven, but now she sat on its edge and held the folded piece of cheap paper to the light.

"I have no right to look," she said, letting her eyes search

79

for words as the paper slowly opened. "It's kind of like a play or a movie and I'm afraid of what I'll find. I might be the cause of hanging someone."

For just a second she hesitated, enjoying the shivers that raced along her spine and the faintness in her chest, then she spread the penciled sheet across her knee and bent over it.

It began, "My darling," and went on in the simple style of a soldier talking to a girl. After the first few sentences Penny blushed with shame at herself and stopped reading. There was nothing wrong in the letter. It was simply Marcia's private life that excluded Terry.

She felt sad at the thought of Terry and his very apparent interest in Marcia, and so she lifted the paper again, and with unreasoning resentment, let her eyes go down the page.

"My darling," (she read again.)

"In spite of your father's objections, I had hoped to be with you longer, to convince you that I love you, and to meet you in California next month. But that's all impossible now, for I won't be going on maneuvers with my outfit. I'm being yanked out in a couple of weeks, Al, Thad, and I. We're to be given some sort of special detail, and later Ike and Tom will join us. They're tough guys, but I understand them and can work with them. I have a ten-day furlough and will go to Virginia to see Mom. So don't stick around here, darling, waiting for me to see you. Your uncle's right —I'm no good. Go back home now and forget me."

The letter bore no signature, and Penny sat with it in her hand, remorseful and ashamed. Tears spilled out of her eyes. She switched off the light to sit in the dark, lost in troubled thought. Often, as a child, she had done that, weighing a misdemeanor or failure to obey her parents; and now, as then, her heart told her she must make amends, and must see that punishment was meted out. But how? It seemed a long time before she could square her shoulders and leave the security of the chaise lounge, to grope her way across her room and along the hall.

"Mums?" she whispered, standing in the door to her mother's room. "Are you and Dad still awake?"

"What is it, darling?" A light snapped on and Mrs. Parrish's tousled head lifted from the pillow of one twin bed while from the other Colonel Parrish shielded his eyes with his arm. "Come in, dear. What's wrong?"

Penny ran the few feet from the door and flung herself on the bed beside her mother. "I've done something awful," she sobbed, "awful, and wrong, and wicked."

"What, Pen?" Colonel Parrish raised himself on an elbow, but Penny was beyond speaking. She only clutched the letter and sobbed convulsively, so he slipped on his dressing gown and came to sit beside her. "What is it, honey?" he asked, trying to pull her out of her mother's arms where she clung. "Tell your dad about it."

"I stole a letter." Penny released her mother's neck and sat up. She rubbed the back of her hand across her eyes, then dropped her tear-stained face on his shoulder and managed to say, "I stole it from Marcia, right out of her glove. And I pretended I hadn't."

"From Marcia McMain?" Each word was alert, and Penny could feel Colonel Parrish stiffen under her weight. But he only asked, "How did you happen to do that, Pen?"

"I thought she was a spy. I've been watching her—and

when I saw a soldier give her a note in the movies I followed her and stole it. But it's only a love letter." Penny raised her head and looked up at him. "I'll have to give it back, Dad, and apologize to her. Perhaps she'll tell people about it and it'll be embarrassing for you. I guess I'd better call her up right away because she was so worried about it."

"Wait a minute." Her father kept his arm around her and held her beside him while her mother sat up and reached for Penny's hand.

"But I did wrong, Dad," she argued. "I have to fix it, right now."

"Yes, you did wrong." Colonel Parrish frowned and sat silently stroking her hair before he asked gently, "Will you let me see the letter before you call Marcia, Pen?"

"Oh, no. It was wrong for even me to read it." She looked down at the crumpled paper and shook her head. "You don't think that would be right, do you? You and Mums have always said . . ."

"I know."

He got up and walked to the window to stand looking out into the night, at the barracks across the parade ground where only a few lights glowed, at the brick hospital building, the sleeping homes. The roar of tanks, moving in long columns on a distant road came to him, and when he turned back to Penny his face was stern. "All right, Pen," he said, "you may as well know it. G2 suspects Marcia of being a spy. So let me have the letter."

"You mean . . . ?" Penny twisted around on the bed and looked at him. "Why, Dad!" she cried in disbelief. "I thought it was sort of exciting to follow her, but . . ."

"You were only play-acting and couldn't quite believe it. I know." For a second his face looked sad, then he held out his hand, and as Penny put the letter into it she realized she had never before seen her father in the role of an officer taking a report from a subordinate.

Without a word he went into his study and lighted the fluorescent lamp on his desk. Penny tossed her mother a robe, and by the time they sped after him, he was already seated and reading rapidly.

"I don't see a thing," Penny whispered to Mrs. Parrish, "except that this is going to make my apologies worse."

They look helplessly at each other, trying to communicate their puzzled thoughts, until Colonel Parrish began jotting initials on a scratch pad and they both bent over to look.

"There it is," he said. "Read it."

Penny leaned closer, but her mother was murmuring, "A.T and I.T. That's what you've written, but what does it mean?"

Colonel Parrish sighed and threw his pencil on the desk. "The whole future of the division is in that letter," he said, "but I don't see how the plans got out."

"What 'got out'? I don't see a thing." Penny hung over the paper, and the eyes of her parents met above her head. The room was still except for the distant roar of the tanks, and her father picked up his pencil again and said, rolling it between his fingers:

"You spotted this thing, Pen, so I suppose you have a right to know. The division is going overseas and this letter tells someone."

"Oh, Dad!"

83

"We're going very soon, and this letter..."

"David, too?"

"Yes."

"And did Mums know?" Penny turned to look at her mother, and when Mrs. Parrish nodded her head, she asked, "When?"

"You can read it for yourself." Colonel Parrish began moving his pencil along the carefully written lines of the letter, and his wife laid her cheek against his hair while she watched him. Penny sat on a corner of the desk, trying to grasp the meaning behind the words he explained, and watching the revelation with amazement.

"If no one had suspected Marcia," he said, "this note would have meant nothing. But as it turns out, it's quite easily deciphered. As you can see, the writer points out that, quite suddenly, he finds he can't go to California. That's true. We had planned to have desert training there before we shipped out; but as he also shows, we'll skip maneuvers and go straight overseas. 'Yanked out,' he says. And he's exact, almost to the day." Colonel Parrish reached up to pat his wife's hand that lay on his shoulder, and pointed to the letter again. "He says that Al and Thad are going with him. Do you get that, Penny?"

"No." Penny shook her head, then cried in surprise, "A.T. A, in Al. T, in Thad. African Theater."

"Right. We're going to train in French Morocco. And for what?"

"For I.T. The Italian Theater."

"Right again. And 'tough guy' means that the division is at full strength and fully equipped. And then comes the sign-off, 'go home.' That's all he has to tell, so pass the word along."

"But wait a minute." Penny bent over the letter again. "You skipped the part where he says he has a ten-day furlough and will go to Virginia. Does that mean. . . ?"

"I hoped you wouldn't notice that line." Colonel Parrish picked up the letter and tapped it thoughtfully. "The rest of the information wouldn't matter so much without that," he said. "The division will be prepared to go to Virginia on maneuvers instead of California, and we'll tell the boys that —for after all, they'll know in what direction they're traveling. But being near Norfolk and the port of embarkation there'll be no commotion when the troops are suddenly loaded onto a transport. Honey, you've done a good piece of work."

Colonel Parrish's eyes were soft as they rested on Penny, but an instant later they were keen and blue again. "I have to find that boy," he said. "I don't think he'll make a run for it until he's sure that Marcia didn't just lose the letter. Do you think you could remember what he looked like?"

"Of course, I've seen him twice. He has red hair."

"Then, get Terry on the phone. I'll talk to him."

Penny rushed into the hall as Bobby appeared in his door, pajama-clad and sleepy. "Go back," she whispered, giving him a push. "I'm having some business with Dad that doesn't concern you. Go *on!*"

She closed his door forcefully, and as she waited for the operator's latent voice, thought excitedly, "I'm helping. I'm helping my country. And perhaps I've saved David's ship from a submarine so he can come back to see his baby."

Up Goes the Curtain

She was excited, too, all through the next hour when her father and the provost marshal were writing down her description of the red-haired soldier, and were instructing military police to guard the roads to Louisville, and had wakened the bewildered hostess of Service Club Number 1. But when she was in bed for the few remaining hours until dawn, she remembered the light that was said to be burning in Marcia's room, and thought of the guard who was standing silently in the corridor. And she wondered if Marcia were suffering. If, behind her locked door, she felt fear and panic.

CHAPTER VII

THERE had been little sleep in the Parrish household that night. Terry had come, officially and in a government car, and Penny had been called down again to repeat her story to him. The phone rang intermittently, and at six o'clock Colonel Parrish had left the house to be seen and heard from no more. The excitement ebbed with Trudy preparing breakfast as usual and with an unsuspecting Tippy going off to school. Bobby, frustrated and curious, pieced out what drama he could, and the house settled down to its usual calm, although Penny stood at the window and fumed.

"It's getting later and later," she complained, "and not a word from Dad about whether I'm to pick up Marcia. If I don't meet her as we'd planned she's going to suspect something."

"He said to wait until they round up the soldier." Carrol, who was helping Bobby eat the late breakfast Trudy had brought for Penny on a tray, said over a piece of toast, "The hostess at the club gave them his name so they should have him by now."

"I'll bet they're putting the screws on him." Bobby bared his teeth and held his knife aloft like a dagger. "Maybe they'll have to *choke* the truth out of him. Gosh, I wish I could've caught him! I'd have knocked him down and put my foot on his neck and. . . ."

"You were right there in the theater with him and all you thought about was your own evening—which reminds me.

87

What did you do with that five dollars I gave you?"

"Five dol . . ."

"Five dollars." Penny turned from the window and went to stand over him. "Even in the excitement I looked in my purse. I had six bucks before I met you and now there's only one nestling in my wallet."

"Well, gee whizz." Bobby twisted on to one hip and pulled four crumpled bills from the disreputable cords he was wearing instead of his trim uniform. "I thought this was a gift," he said sadly, holding them out. "Sort of a homecoming present."

"Not a chance." Penny took the bills, smoothed them out, then gave one back to him. "Maybe it is," she said, putting the others in a bon bon dish, "but watch out how you spend it. Oh, dear, I do wish Dad would phone."

"It's hard to be on the wrong end of the line." Carrol got up and followed her back to the window. "Something may be happening in headquarters," she said, looking out at the three-storied brick building which, with the theater, bordered one side of the parade ground. "Do you suppose, if we stand here we could watch someone go in or out?"

"I don't think so. I think all the excitement's out at Division Headquarters. We might drive out there."

"We can't. Suppose your father should call."

"I considered that. He wouldn't have to if I were sitting right where he could reach me. Shall we?"

"I'm going, too." Bobby prepared to rise, which meant shifting from his spine and untangling his legs, but Carrol shook her head at him. "We'll stay here a little longer," she decided. "If. . . ."

Up Goes the Curtain

The telephone rang and Penny shot into the hall. Her heart was pounding when she lifted the receiver and when her father's voice said, "Everything's all right and we have the boy," she collapsed on the nearest chair.

"Did he confess?" she asked.

"Yes. We've been holding an investigation this morning, and I'll tell you what I can when I come home to lunch."

"But what about Marcia?" Penny cried, afraid he would hang up. "Shall I meet her?"

"She's been here; there's nothing more for you to do, honey."

"Oh." Penny hung up the telephone with great disappointment. Life seemed dull without her work of espionage, and she went soberly back into the living room. "It's all over," she said, flopping into a chair. "And just because I'm not in the army, I'm going to miss all the excitement at the end. Dad even said 'I'll tell you what I can'—and that may not be much."

"But, darling, you did catch them, you know." Carrol watched Bobby go off to relay the news to his mother, and added, "Think what it means to me, Penny, just one person. Suppose the Germans should be on the watch for our convoy. Why, it means everything to me!" And think of all the other wives and mothers—think of Mums!"

"Oh, lamb," Penny bounced up and hurled herself onto the arm of Carrol's chair, "I forgot all about you and the fact that David's going away, David and Dad and his regiment. Did you know about it before?"

"I knew they were going, but not when. I had to know that much because—well, I had to buy so many things for

David. Razor blades and a fur cap and new undershirts."
Carrol smiled reminiscently. "We just pretended he was
going on maneuvers in a fur cap," she added, "but I knew."

"I guess wives have a sort of sixth sense or something,"
Penny answered. "They just go on as if nothing were happening." And then she said, still a little cross with David,
"And I suppose that's why you behaved so beautifully when
he went overboard about Marcia."

"David didn't go overboard." Carrol had to laugh, but she
explained simply, "He was only helping Terry."

"How do you know that?" Penny looked incredulous
but, as Carrol clarified David's part in the trap Terry had
tried to lay for Marcia, a reluctant grin spread across her face
and she admitted sheepishly, "I must have acted like a nut."

"Well, whatever you acted like, you did what the G2
Department couldn't; you caught the gal."

"Say, I did, didn't I?" Penny sat up straighter. "My goodness, maybe I'd better join the WACs or hire myself out to
the F.B.I."

"I'd rest on my laurels."

Carrol had a mental picture of Penny sleuthing; trailing
anyone who acted strangely or who failed to arouse her admiration; and as she might quite conceivably end in jail herself, she was, Carrol decided, safer behind the footlights,
playing a part that was written for her by someone else. So
she led the conversation to the theater and suddenly it was
time for lunch and Colonel Parrish was standing in the hall.

"Tell us everything quickly!" Penny cried, swinging on
his neck so that David, who was trying to get in the door,
gave them a bump. "What did you do to them?"

Up Goes the Curtain

"Not so fast." Her father hung his coat over the newel post, a favorite act through his twenty-five years of military service, and one that always brought his wife to remove it. Now she waited for the two overseas caps and the short tank jackets, then hung them in the coat closet where they belonged.

"We'd better go upstairs," Colonel Parrish said, grinning at her with the small boy apology that was part of the ritual. "There's no use for Trudy and Tip to be in on this. Did Bobby stay in the house and keep mum as I told him to do?"

"Never a word, sir." The sleek and resplendent cadet in full regalia who saluted them from above made them all laugh, and Bobby said gruffly before he disappeared, "Thought I might as well be military."

"Oh, quite, old chap." David's eyes twinkled and he stepped back to motion grandly, "Let us proceed according to rank. Mums, on your way. Detective Parrish—Mrs. Parrish, Junior—Dad—and I as a lowly captain will bring up the rear. Attention, up there, Corporal."

It was a dignified procession that started up the stairs, but when they reached the top they raced for seats in Colonel Parrish's study, and he, as the last one in, closed the door and leaned against it. "All right," he said. "Where do you want me to start?"

"With what happened this morning." Penny had managed her favorite place on the corner of his desk, and she reached out to pull him into his worn leather chair, then leaned forward and asked, "Is Marcia in the guardhouse?"

"No, she was giving testimony when I came home." He turned the chair until it faced the room and said carefully,

"The plot went far deeper than any of you have suspected. Marcia and the soldier, Carl Sommers, were only the go-betweens. The head of it, so far as Fort Knox is concerned, is an officer in my regiment; a man I've always considered efficient, and smart. Major Beckman. He got the information and passed it on."

"He was smart, all right," David growled, while Mrs. Parrish exclaimed,

"Major Beckman! Why, Dave, I've always liked him—he came here to dine once." And then she broke off to ask, "But why did he have to have someone to *tell* things to? Couldn't he have passed them on himself?"

"That was too dangerous and too easily checked. Beckman gave the news to a soldier, and the soldier passed it on to different girls who came to stay on the post. Miss Cox at the Service Club says that Marcia has been out here several times this past winter, pretending to call on her cousin. She had a little trouble recognizing the girl today."

"I don't wonder," Penny put in. "When she went there she had her hair down and no make-up or eyelashes on, and the day I saw her she was wearing a suit with a pleated skirt, college girl type."

"We showed Miss Cox her clothes."

"And did Marcia admit anything?"

"In a way, yes. But she said . . ."

"Wait a minute." Penny, who had appointed herself to conduct the inquisition, slid forward on the desk and asked eagerly, "Did she know Major Beckman?"

"Yes, she said she did."

"Then I'll bet she's married to him. She is, isn't she?"

"Oh, Penny, for goodness' sake!" her mother exclaimed. "You're always hunting for romance. German sympathizers don't have to be *married* to be spies."

"Well, I'll bet she is. Is she, Dad?"

Her father smiled and laid his arm across her knee. "That's her story," he said. "She has taken the line that she's married to Beckman but is in love with the soldier, and that that's all there is to it."

"I knew it!" Penny bounced about on the desk, quite pleased with her intuition, but stopped to frown when Carrol asked,

"How did Major Beckman come in the picture? Did Marcia implicate him?"

"No," Colonel Parrish smiled at her and teased Penny by saying, "A very good question and more to the point than the one about Marcia's marriage. The soldier, Sommers, vowed he hardly knew Marcia and hadn't written the note. Unfortunately, for him, we found a scratch pad in his foot locker that bore identical pencil prints on its first page. Confronted with that, he became rattled, got Beckman into the picture, hoping to save himself, and of course, gave us a web of facts to untangle."

"Hm." Penny scowled down at her clasped hands and blinked in concentration. She knew that at any moment her father might consider the matter closed, since he hadn't her fondness for details, so she asked the first question she could think of that would keep him talking. "Was the great Hayes shocked to bits?"

"He was no end pleased."

"Then perhaps he wasn't as crazy about Marcia as he seemed. Though he did act like it."

"So did David. Remember?" Carrol laughed and added, "He fooled you, too." David reached out for her hand and as she looked down at the two clasped tightly together she sighed and said softly, "Poor Marcia. What will happen to her, Dad?"

"She'll be interned, I suppose, and put where she can't do any more harm. Not being in the army, she'll be turned over to the federal authorities."

"And the soldier? And Major Beckman?"

"That I can't tell you. They'll have courts martial for treason, you know."

There was silence in the room as each one sat thinking of the penalty traitors must pay, until Bobby, awed and a little frightened, rubbed his stubby head and said, "Gosh." At which his father looked at him and instructed sternly:

"You remember what I told you, Bob?"

"Yes, sir."

"You're not to talk until this thing is over, until we're sure we have caught all the criminals. That's clear, isn't it?"

"Yes, sir, but I guess I'd better sort of hang around home today, maybe." Bobby looked pleadingly at Carrol, then Penny. "Could I kind of be with you?" he asked.

"All day." Carrol made room for him on the couch and he eased in between her and David like a small tug into its dock, glad to know that large liners were berthed on either side of it.

"And now let's have lunch. I'm hungry." Colonel Parrish

94

stood up and shook his head warningly as they filed out the door. "No more conversation," he whispered. "We're back to everyday living."

"Okay." Bobby swept past him on the banister rail. He collided with a bewildered Tippy at the bottom, attacked his lunch with the hungry gusto of a fireman stoking a furnace, but when his father pushed back his chair and said to Mrs. Parrish, "If you want the car this afternoon the girls will have to drive me out to the regiment," he was on his feet and asking, "Can I go too, Pen?"

"Sure, but don't talk all the time." Penny gave him a push toward the hall, but as they went across the lawn to the car in the driveway, Carrol put her arm around his shoulders and they strolled along together.

She had never recovered from the wonder of having so many brothers and sisters, and, because of a lonely childhood, was constantly giving herself mental pinches that kept her awake to her great good fortune. So she climbed into her own car beside David and pulled Bobby in with her. She loved the pressure of David's arm in its olive drab sleeve on one side of her and the bonier structure in cadet gray on the other, and she called out the window to Penny:

"You can deliver your father, then pick Bobby and me up at Headquarters." Penny nodded, so she settled back with a hand on each of the knees beside her.

The drive along roads that twisted and turned through a labyrinth of wooden buildings, barracks, machine shops, and tank sheds, seemed to take but a second, and when David kissed her good-by and left her before a large two-storied building, she stood in the gravel and watched Bobby teeter on the whitewashed stones that marked the semi-circular drive.

"Look," she motioned as a government car whisked in across from them and stopped before the steps. "Do you suppose those two men in civilian clothes are from the F.B.I.?"

"Sure." Bobby flailed his arms for balance while he stared, then hopped off the rock. "Gosh. Let's stay here all afternoon and see what happens!" he cried.

"We can't, because your mother needs the car." Carrol saw Penny bowling toward them and waved for her to stop in the road while she and Bobby ran to her.

"See that car that's backing into the wide place in front of the door?" Bobby pointed, climbing into the back seat of the sedan. "Two F.B.I. guys got out of it."

"Really?" Penny turned off the motor and the three sat watching.

"They looked like F.B.I.," Carrol explained, "and what would civilians be doing riding around in a government car? And why would the driver be waiting?"

"Let's sit here awhile and find out." Penny leaned across Carrol to crank the window, and Bobby pressed his nose against the glass behind him.

"But they may be in there all afternoon, and your mother wants the car."

"If they were going to stay too long the driver wouldn't park; he'd come back. Let's try it until two o'clock, anyway."

The minutes dragged by slowly, with officers entering and leaving the building, and when Penny was looking at her watch for the last time, Carrol saw the soldier in the official car straighten up, lay aside his magazine, and start his motor.

"Hold it," she said. "He can see something in the center hall that we can't."

With a spurt of gravel, the car pulled up before the door again, blocking their view, and in a flash Penny had turned her own key and was backing a few feet.

"Heavens above, I wish you'd look!" she cried, yanking on her emergency brake so that they all shot forward. "There she *is!*"

Marcia was coming slowly down the steps between the two government men. Her black hair was as smooth as ever, her trimly fitted black suit as smart; but even though she held her head high, there was a look of strain and weariness about her.

"She must be glad it's all over," Carrol said, watching one of the men step into the car while the other waited for Marcia to get in beside him. "She had to know that someday she'd be caught."

"I guess she did. But think how low and terrible she feels to have betrayed her country. And to have people staring at her and hating her. But perhaps she's too hard to care. She'd have to be if she didn't mind killing thousands of our boys. She's horrible."

Marcia was sitting very straight between the two men and, as the car pulled out, Bobby asked, "Where do you suppose they're taking her?"

"To the train in Louisville perhaps, and then to Washington maybe, or to New York, if that's her state." Penny was thoughtful for a moment, then she added, "I wish they would stand her up and tie her right out in front of The

White House, or perhaps the Capitol, or the Supreme Court of Justice where everyone could see her. Being a spy wouldn't look so glamourous then, would it?"

"No." Carrol's eyes were following the car on the road ahead of them. She saw Penny lean forward to release her brake, but, before she could touch it, reached out to put both arms around her. "Oh, Penny," she whispered, "thank you."

CHAPTER VIII

"Miss Penny? There's a gen'man downstairs to see you." Trudy stood in the doorway grinning broadly, and Penny turned from the dressing table and stopped combing her hair.

"To see me?" she repeated. "Who is it?"

"Law," Trudy chuckled comfortably and came a little inside. "Who do you reckon would come a'callin' at four o'clock on a Sunday afternoon? Mr. Terry."

"Oh, my." Penny looked surprised and Trudy whispered complacently, "Everybody scattered out of the living room like chickens out of a coop. Yo' mamma and papa said 'howdy-do' and that they was jes' starting fo' a walk, an' Tippy had to pick up her paper dolls, an' Bobby ..."

"What's the matter with him, with Terry, I mean? Is he mad at me for being the one to catch Marcia?"

"Do he look mad, holdin' a box that's gotta be candy in one hand an' one that's gotta be flowers in the other?" Trudy enjoyed the pleased embarrassment that spread over Penny's face, and added slyly, "He's courtin', honey."

"Pooh." Penny threw down the comb and dusted powder from her red crepe jumper. "He's only trying to make peace, like he's done dozens of times before. He always hates it when I get the best of him, and I usually do. I'll go down and pacify him."

But she was a little shy when she entered the living room and tried to say a casual "Hello." Terry had laid his packages

99

on a table and was standing in the middle of the room, watching for her.

"Penny," he said simply, going to her and taking her by the shoulders, "will you forgive me? I wanted to come over last night and ask you but I had to go to Louisville. I've had a bad week, Pen."

"Why. . . ." Penny's gift for light repartee deserted her, and she looked helplessly at him. "You didn't do anything," she admitted honestly, a little frightened at the truth. "I didn't mind."

"Didn't it matter to you that Marcia seemed to have come here to see me, and that I wanted her here?"

"Oh, Terry," Penny eased herself from between his hands and stepped back from him, "I didn't think much about it, that way. Of course, I was kind of mad at you, and at David and Marcia, too, but—Terry, if I have to tell you, I guess I'll have to. I didn't really *suffer* much."

"So that's the way it is." Terry's jaw tightened and Penny saw a little ripple of muscles run along it. "I suppose I should have known," he said, his blue eyes steady on her upraised brown ones. "Is it Mike Drayton, Pen?"

"No." Penny smiled and shook her head. "Michael is grand!" she explained. "He's been a friend of David's and mine ever since we were little children, and he was wonderful to me while he was David's roommate at the Point; but, Terry—it just isn't anybody. I told Michael that, too, before he flew his bomber to England. I'm not in love with anyone; really in love, so that nothing else matters. If I were. . . ."

"Would I be the one, Pen?"

She turned to face the window without answering, and

after waiting a moment Terry laid the tip of his finger against her cheek and brought her back to him. "Would I, Pen?" he asked gently.

"I honestly don't know. I don't let myself think seriously about love," she said, "because it seems women can't have a career and go dashing around to army posts with their husbands at the same time."

"What if a girl should marry out of the army?"

"Why, *Terry!* Who'd ever marry out of the army!" There was such shocked surprise on Penny's face that he smiled in spite of the ache in his heart, and put both arms around her.

"It's all right, lamb-child," he said, with his cheek against the fragrance of her hair. "Take your time, but don't put me out of your heart completely, will you?"

"Never, Terry." Penny clung to him a little, afraid for the good-by they were saying, and wondering—will I regret it someday? If something should happen to him in the war, or if he should find some other girl to love, will I be sorry?

She sighed, with her cheek resting against the row of ribbons on his chest, but before two tears could squeeze between her closed eyelids, he pulled her head back and grinned down at her.

"Take it easy, lamb," he said. "I wouldn't marry you until the war's over, anyway. I just thought a diamond ring would sparkle pretty on your finger."

"Truly, Terry?"

"Truly, darling."

"And you're not unhappy? You're not—not *depressed?*"

Terry threw back his head and laughed at her choice of a

word. "I'm not depressed," he assured her, giving her such a quick hug that her breath went out in a cough, "although I'm pressed as flat inside as you are now—with chagrin, because you beat me on Marcia. You're a demon, Penny."

"But you don't really mind." She wriggled to get free, then, still in the circle of his arms, reached up to take his cheeks between her hands. "You know, don't you, that I want you to be the one I love someday?" she asked, so childishly sincere that he knew love hadn't yet come to Penny.

"Thanks, lamb-child," he said, opening one of her hands and putting a kiss in it, then closing it into a fist. "We'll talk this over again in about a year from now. Will you drive in to the train with me tonight?"

"Could I? Mums and Dad are sending Bobby off at nine o'clock and I can come back with them."

"Swell! And since I won't have to keep a driver waiting to bring you home, suppose we order a car now and have dinner in town. We can grab a taxi from the hotel to the station—and you certainly should go some place to wear the orchids I brought you."

"Orchids? Oh, joy!" Penny ran to the florist box and jerked off the lid. "You sent me orchids once before," she said impudently, "after I had outwitted you."

"Oh, no, I didn't. They were to express my regret and compassion for having been the winner in that fight," he protested . "It seems to me that we've exchanged several orchids in our lives. You sent me one, once, that arrived when I was with a crowd of officers, and that humiliated me no end."

"And you retaliated by throwing it at me." They were on

familiar ground now, and Penny pinned the purple blooms on her red dress, then shuddered at the color combination and took them off. "I'll have to change," she said. "Why don't you call down the hall to Trudy's room and heckle her into making us some coffee and cinnamon toast? She'll do it for you."

"Of course, she will. Trudy loves me; she appreciates me."

"I do, too." Penny walked with him into the hall, and then, a few steps up on the stairway hung over the banister rail. "I can have more fun with you than with any man I know," she said.

"That's fine. That's just dandy." Terry leaned an elbow on the newel post and regarded her darkly. "That should make my life complete," he remarked with such sarcasm that she stepped back.

"Oh, Terry," she began, "I didn't mean. . . ."

"Scat!" His grin flashed out and his arm swept through the air so that she ran, laughing and relieved to hear him going along the hall shouting, "Trudy? Hey, Trudy, come out."

They had a delightful time in Louisville, and when the train was ready to leave he called down from the vestibule door, "I'll phone you one night next week, and I'll be in New York to see you as soon as I can."

She waved gayly to him, but with a sadness too, one that stayed with her when she was homeward-bound with her parents. Colonel and Mrs. Parrish were quiet, and Penny leaned forward to rest her chin on the back of the front seat. "Where do we go from here?" she asked.

"Hm?" Her mother turned around, surprised at the voice that came from so near, and said with a smile, "It looks as if we scatter a bit."

"How do you mean?"

"Well," Colonel Parrish pulled a cigarette from his case and pushed in the lighter on the dash, "David and I have to shove on," he said casually, holding the glowing electric coil to his cigarette while Penny waited. "Your mother can stay on in the house for a month, which will take Tippy near enough to the end of the term for her to pass, and they can visit the relatives in Chicago until Bobby is through."

"But, Penny," Marjorie Parrish said slowly, "we think Carrol should go back with you, just as soon as David goes, even if you have to leave a day or two earlier."

"I do, too." Penny pushed her mother gently aside and climbed over the seat between them. A few sparks flew from her father's cigarette and the orchids were beyond saving, but she wedged herself in the middle and linked her arms through theirs. "Carrol shouldn't be left in that house," she said, not noticing that Mrs. Parrish was trying to put her hat back on.

"And she and David mustn't have their last memories ruined by crates and barrels and excelsior," her father declared. "So your mother suggested they live in their little house, just as they are, until they lock their door behind them. Then she'll go over with the packers and move their stuff out."

"Oh, Mums, that's sweet." Penny hugged close to her mother. "I'll love having Carrol go back with me," she said, "but I hate to leave you here, alone. I can stay if you want me to."

"I don't. I'd much rather you'd take Carrol away. I've gone through two wars and I remember how utterly lost I felt when your father left me in a hotel in New York when he went off to the last one. I have Tippy and Bobby, now, and would rather be right in my own dear house where Dad won't have to worry about us until it's time for us to go east to be with you and Carrol."

"Have you talked with Carrol about it?"

"Not yet. I put out a few feelers, and Dad did too, with David; but it's hard to interfere. We thought you might suggest it in the morning, just as if it's an idea you could work out together."

"All right." Penny slid farther down into her seat, watching the headlights seek out dark shadows along the side of the road and listening to her parents casually planning their future. Sometimes they talked across her and sometimes she entered into their discussions, but they were eager and enthusiastic about all they were going to do, and as gay as if Colonel Parrish were going on a vacation cruise while his wife went east for the summer.

"I don't see how you two do it," Penny said, just as they reached home. "Me, I'd be streaming tears all over the place."

"You aren't." Her father grinned at her and let the car coast into the garage.

"But I have things to look forward to. I'll be busy."

"So will your mother and I. And we'll look forward to

being together again. This isn't half as bad as when we did it before."

"Isn't it?"

"No, we're a family now; and you can't separate a family. Remember that, Pen. I'll be with you all the time, and you'll be with me."

"I guess that's true. It was that way when you flew to England last year."

"I'm going to miss Dad," her mother said, opening the door but sitting still while it swung back, "but I have such faith in him. I know his ability, his strength, his power to make the right decisions and to take care of his men. David's the one I'll worry about, because he's still a boy who needs us."

"I'll look after him for you." Colonel Parrish patted her knee and said jokingly, "Carrol might resent your speaking so slightingly of her fine strong husband."

Marjorie Parrish laughed and climbed out of the car. "She undoubtedly would." And then she held out a hand to Penny and urged, "Go over early, dear, and coax her to leave with you."

"I'm always there early, and I'll fix it." Penny answered with pert assurance. But the next morning, when she was watching Carrol put some of David's wool socks on stretchers, she wondered how to broach the subject; and Carrol was standing the stretchers in a row along the sink before she gave up the idea of a roundabout course, and plunged in.

"Would you like to go to New York with me?" she asked.

"Just lock up the house, tell David good-by, and get on the train?"

"That's what I'm planning to do." Carrol smoothed a wrinkle from one of the olive drab socks and when she looked around, Penny was sitting on a stool with her mouth open. "Don't look so stunned," she laughed. "David and I aren't deaf, dumb, and blind. Dad throws out a few hints to David, Mums suggests in circles to me. We put our heads together and David decides it. Pfft—just like that."

"Well!"

"He makes reservations for a drawing-room, for you and me; arranges with the quartermaster to send packers on a certain day; and telephones Miss Turner to have the apartment in order because I'll be in New York for a few days on business. I'll tell the servants the truth after he's gone."

"David did all that?"

"Well, of course. You know, Penny," Carrol explained carefully, "David's a man. He not only plans for me, but his battalion's lucky to have him for a commander. I wish I could go out and tell them how lucky they are."

"Oh, my goodness." Penny, on her stool, exploded with laughter. "And Mums said he's a boy, and is worried, and Dad promised to take care of him! Oh, Carrol, you're priceless."

"I'm not, I'm just lucky. I'd trust David with my life; and I'd trust him in a crisis before I would Dad. Because he's younger and can think and move faster."

Penny rocked with mirth at the picture her mother and father had painted of poor devastated little Carrol and helpless little David. "I guess our generation's pretty darn good," she said. "We go at things hammer and tongs, and get the job done."

"I hope we do" Carrol looked thoughtful as she led the way into the living room. "I hope David will finish things so our son won't have to do it all over again." And then she pointed to some boxes on the divan and said in a gay, light tone, "His fine layette came today. I wanted David to see all his clothes so I can write, 'Davie wore the pink silk bonnet and coat today,' and then he'll know how ridiculous the poor baby looked, and how mad."

"What did he say about the stuff?"

"He thought it was cute." Carrol lifted the lid of one of the boxes and took out the pink silk bonnet, and smoothed it.

"Madam," David had said, walking around the room with the bonnet on top of his head, the ribbons knotted under his chin, "this is the way I looked in my babyhood. Do you think any girl will ever fall in love with our son?"

"No." Carrol, on her knees before the boxes, pulled out a small white dress. "And this is the way I looked," she said, laying it over her chest. "Would you have cared for me in a style like this?"

"Never. I'd have been ashamed to be seen with such a sissy. What else have we to try on?"

He dropped down beside her, and before they had finished exploring, their fingers were gloved in small bootees and the chairs were strewn with diminutive clothes.

"Poor little kid," David said, sitting on the floor and kissing Carrol. "Why don't you put the stuff fancily away in drawers and let him be comfortable in his pants and a shirt?"

"Shall I?"

"Sure. I'd kind of like to have a girl who looks like you, but I'd hate to wish all this stuff on her."

"We'll get Davie a little sister sometime," she answered, "but these things are for him."

Now she smiled at Penny, smoothed the bonnet, and repeated softly, "David thought they were cute."

CHAPTER IX

Twelve days flew by on wings, with dawn crowding the full, pure moon from the sky, and with night throwing a blanket over the sun long before it seemed time for it to go to rest. The post was mildly excited that a spy had been caught in its midst, but few people knew that the division's maneuvers would terminate at the end of ten days; and those few guarded the secret carefully. Penny spent her days with Carrol, planning their life in New York, but was content to be at home in the evenings and at·work on her script of *The Robin's Nest*, leaving Carrol and David their privacy. And at last the luggage was packed, Carrol's trunks had been shipped, and David was giving her the envelope that held her ticket.

"It's better this way, darling," he said, watching her tuck the envelope into her purse. "I want to put you on the train and know you're safely on your way. I can come back and load up the troop train tomorrow with an easier mind, and I can talk to you on the phone before we have to pull out."

"I know." Carrol's lips trembled a little as she bent over a stubborn zipper on her purse, but the tremble turned into a smile when she looked up. "If you can get a twenty-four hour pass, you'll come up to New York, won't you?" she asked.

"You know I will. And Dad thinks he can work it for me. He's pretty sure that some of us can have even a week-end, and says it all depends on how lucky I am at drawing the right piece of paper out of a hat. But I'll get at least twenty-four hours, you can bet."

"What if you only draw twelve?"

"Then I'll wire you to come halfway. We'll be together again, dearest, I promise that."

David put his arm around her, and together, without a word, they walked through their tiny house. In the kitchen she ran her hand tenderly along the rim of the sink and David took it in his and kissed a burn on one finger. The trip through the dining-room, between the table and wall, was too narrow to manage side by side and they laughed when he pushed her ahead of him; but back in the living room they clung together until David said, "Okay, sweet," and picked up her coat.

From then on it was a jumble of events. Excitement reigned at the Parrishes, with Penny alternately kissing everyone or splashing tears on her father's blouse.

"Don't let's go but just say we did," she groaned, hugging Tippy and Trudy, then getting into the car. "I love coming home, but I hate going away. I think Mums and Carrol and I should take knock-out drops that would last till the war's over."

"And miss David's letters? No, thanks." Carrol laughed, but when she was on the station platform she walked through the gates to the train beside David and whispered, "Don't go back into our house, will you? Not once. Promise?"

"I won't go in, sweet. I couldn't take it."

"Everything you'll need is at Mums', and I put the six new toothbrushes in your shaving kit."

"Thanks, dearest."

The others went on into the drawing room but David stopped Carrol in the corridor. "We've been happy, haven't we?" he whispered, holding her close. "You'll never be out of my thoughts. Always know, Carrol, that I love you so much I'm sure I'm coming home to you."

"I'm sure of it, too, David. You aren't even leaving me."

"And I'll see you in a few days in New York. We'll go on the town. We'll hunt up every dance band we knew when I was in the Point, and we'll have a swell time, only it'll be more fun, now."

He tipped her face up and grinned down at her. "Good-by—wife," he said with the special little wink he kept for her, just as Colonel and Mrs. Parrish came into the narrow aisle and the porter called, "Time to get off, sir."

There was only a moment for David to give a hasty clutch at Penny, whispering, "Take care of her for me." Then the train began to move, and he jumped off to run beside it for a few yards, memorizing Carrol's face as she smiled down at him. But at last he stopped and turned back to walk beside his mother and father, and to say as cheerfully as he could:

"Oh, well, I'll be seeing her in about a week."

Colonel Parrish laid a hand on his shoulder and David turned his head with a jerk. "Won't I?" he asked.

"I'm afraid not, son. Beckman and Marcia forced us to change some plans last night."

David whirled on the platform and stared at the empty tracks where the train had been. "I wouldn't have let her go if I'd known," he said. "Even one more day here would have helped."

"It's better this way, dear." His mother took him by the arm and walked along slowly beside him. "The thought of seeing each other again made the good-bys easier. Carrol isn't as unhappy as she would be had she known this was a final parting. She can make plans and hope, you know."

"I suppose so. But darn it, I still wouldn't have let her go."

On the train, Penny was disposing of their hats and hanging up their coats. "We're very stylish in here, aren't we?" she chattered. "Would you like to go in for a second breakfast?"

"I don't think so." Carrol had to swallow a lump in her throat to answer, and she was afraid to look through the window at the streets where men and women were going about their daily living lest the tears that ached so unbearably behind her eyeballs should break through and gush wildly forth. So she watched Penny climb up to the racks and down again, and sat with her hands locked tightly together while the small room was put in order. It seemed an endless time before the pain in her chest and eyes subsided enough for her to speak; but when the train was rolling through the green hills, she got up and said casually, "Look, pet, if you'd put the purses on top of the magazines—so, things wouldn't slide around so much."

After that it was easier. The day passed and the train tore through the night. Morning came with Penny looking down from the upper berth, and soon it was time to have breakfast and get off.

"From rags to riches," Penny remarked, when she was seated in Carrol's limousine, with the chauffeur, Parker, at the wheel. "It must seem strange to you, after Knox."

"I'd trade every bit of it for more of these." Carrol held up her ungloved finger with the burn David had kissed. "I—I don't belong here anymore, Pen."

But she showed great interest in Parker's family, in the doorman, and in the old man who had run the elevator since she was a child; and when the servants clustered around her, she shook hands with them all and kissed Miss Turner.

"Welcome home, my dear," Miss Turner said in her tiny fluttery voice. "We've missed you very much even though we've had Penny to liven us up."

"I've missed you, too," Carrol answered, smiling a little at the stiff formality of Perkins who was directing the disposal of the luggage.

It all seemed so different from the casual life at Fort Knox, and she yearned for the cheerful whistling of the colored soldier David paid to come in the evening, to shine the boots and shoes and scrub the kitchen linoleum. But the servants were going off about their duties and Penny was exclaiming:

"Do you know something? This is the day I told Letty I'd hunt her up. Do you want to come along?"

She had explained Letty in great detail, so now Carrol shook her head, but said, "Bring her home to dinner if you can. I want to be here if David should call."

"Do you think this—this magnitude would scare her?" Penny waved a hand and Carrol laughed.

"It shouldn't, if it doesn't scare us," she answered, looking through doors at the great expanse of rooms. "Though it is a huge barn of a place, isn't it? I wonder how Daddy and I ever rattled around in it."

"Very comfortably, I may say." Penny, completely at

home, was on her way to the library and called back over her shoulder, "I'll just phone Miss Ware to find out about rehearsals, then I'll whip out and look up Letty."

"And I'll see about the unpacking."

"Okay." Penny was happy at the telephone. She loved hearing Janice Ware tell her that rehearsals would start the following Monday, and jotting down the hour and name of the theater where she would report.

"I'm to go right down the alley," she told Carrol, "to the stage door, like a real actress. Hot dawg! Now I'll find Letty and invite her to dinner."

She went rushing off, excited over the activity that made New York so dear to her, and when she slid onto the stool in the drug store it was as if she had never been away. Letty was plying her wet cloth along the counter and she glanced at Penny without interest, looked away, then jerked back again.

"Well, hello," she said. "So you're back."

"Of course." Penny leaned her elbows on the counter and grinned. "Didn't I say I would, and today?"

"Yeah, but I didn't expect you, and sort of quit thinking about you." Letty saw the hurt look on Penny's face and made an extra sweep with her cloth, sorry for the words her pride had forced her to say; for rarely had a day passed without the hope that Penny would return to give her a glimpse into the glamourous world of which she had written to Joe.

"Why, my goodness, Letty," Penny said with a bewildered shake of her head, "we planned to celebrate today and

I've such a lot to tell you and you promised to come home to dinner with me."

"Oh, I couldn't, really. I have to work."

"But you said you'd take the afternoon off."

"Well. . . ." Letty looked down at her blue uniform and thought of her best black dress that was hanging in her locker; of her new pumps and a flower hat. She had felt foolish, wearing them to work that morning in the vain hope of Penny's return, and had been sure she would only sit alone in a movie, wrinkling the dress and holding the flower hat on her lap. "It's nice of you," she began, "but. . . ."

"Oh, come on." Penny swished off her stool and asked, "Will the manager let you off?"

"I'm through at twelve."

"Then, let's go. It's five after, now."

"I'll have to change my clothes."

Letty sent the wet cloth back into its watery grave and disappeared through a door while Penny inspected the amazing wares of the drug store. She was rounding a counter on her second tour when she saw a very attractive girl regarding her, and exclaimed in amazement:

"Why, Letty, you're *pretty!*"

Letty's clothes were right. Penny could see that out of the corner of her eye as they walked along. They were inexpensive, almost cheap, but her knee-length black coat was plain and her little flower hat had taken a good bit from her savings. They talked endlessly, about Joe, about David and Carrol, and without too much detail, about the spying of Marcia. Letty was silent going up in the elevator, but when

Up Goes the Curtain

Carrol met them in the hall and held out her hand, saying, "Hello, Letty. I hoped Penny could find you," she relaxed to become her cheerful happy self again.

I'll have a lot to tell Joe, she thought, letting her eyes sweep around Carrol's bedroom and into the dressing room and sitting room beyond; and watching Penny apply fresh lipstick while Carrol told of having talked to Mrs. Parrish on the telephone.

"David hadn't come in yet," Carrol said, dropping into a chair beside Letty and leaning forward to ask abruptly, "How do you ever stand it? Does the loneliness get better?"

"Not much. You just—just go on."

The two girls forgot Penny for they had David and Joe. And she sat on the ruffled dressing table stool, feeling lonely, until she remembered her part in the play and went off to get it. She studied her lines for half an hour, and when she came back Carrol was curled up on the bed, talking with David.

"Oh, will you really call once more?" she was saying while Letty held up a warning finger to Penny. "I'll sit up all night and wait. Of course, I'm all right, except that I'm lonely. Oh, David, I love you so much. I know you do. Good-by."

She dropped the telephone into its cradle and leaned her head against the back of the bed. "That was David," she said rapturously.

"Do tell." Penny ran across the room to kiss her. "Does he still miss you, and will I have a chance to talk to him and to Dad tonight?" she asked.

"He said so. They won't pull out until morning and they'll call us. And now, let's have dinner."

Carrol got up from the bed and said as they went along the hall, "You've done me such a lot of good, Letty, because you have so much courage."

"There isn't anything else you can have," Letty answered, going down the stairs and admiring the paintings on the wall. "Courage is kind of like a bank account—you have to save it up for the boys to draw on when they need it."

CHAPTER X

PENNY arose at dawn on Monday morning.
"What do you think I should wear?" she asked, coming into Carrol's room from the one to which she had transferred herself and her belongings in order to practice at odd hours in the night. "I'm in such a twitchet I can't make up my mind. I want to make a good impression so I've tried on everything I own."

"Why, wear your tan suit, of course, and take your plaid topcoat." Carrol looked up from the breakfast she was luxuriously having in bed, but Penny still seemed doubtful.

"It isn't very dressy," she pointed out, leaning against the door. "Maybe my blue sheer and fur jacket would look better."

"You aren't going to a luncheon, my pet; you're going to work. If it's cold in the theater your suit's the thing, and if there's heat on, you can strip down to your blouse and be comfortable." Carrol pushed her bed tray back and looked at the enameled clock on her table. "David should be almost there now," she said.

"I wish *I* could go to some far place." Penny sighed, then executed an exuberant tap step and bolted. "I'll wear the suit," she called back. "I knew you'd tell me to."

She felt very important walking along Broadway and turning into Forty-fourth Street with its double row of theaters. She even walked along a narrow alley with her head high, proud to be one who had a right to drop out of the throng of pedestrians and traverse its narrow runway. But at an inconspicuous weather-scarred door with a light above it, she stopped to get her breath and courage.

"Going in?" a gruff voice behind her asked, as a young man in baggy tweeds reached across her for the door-handle.

"Yes, I am."

He was dark and disheveled, with a black lock of hair that hung from his hatless head over a bony forehead; and had he been taller and browner, would have had the lined, rangy look that is often attractive. But minus those additional attributes, he stared at Penny with deep-set gray eyes, and ducking under his arm, she noticed that his nondescript string of a tie was crooked, as if he had jerked at it.

The nervous type, she catalogued him, walking into the dim theater and making her way to the stage which was adequately lighted and had a number of people sitting about on folding chairs. A few were reading their scripts; several, who had known each other before, were gathered in a little group; but as none glanced toward her and as Miss Ware was nowhere to be seen, Penny chose a chair and sat down.

The stage was a vast place, with flats of scenery stacked along its back wall, with a huddle of furniture at one side, covered with a tarpaulin that let the gilt legs of chairs and a red velvet ottoman show. Corridors led off to the dressing rooms; and after Penny had enjoyed the ugly drabness of the place and had sniffed its satisfying mustiness that never saw the light of day, she let her eyes swing upward to the mass of ropes and pulleys which could raise or lower backdrops and teasers, and watched a man on a narrow catwalk who was mending a cable. The theater would house a musical comedy when it came in from its tryout tour and so would belong to *The Robin's Nest* for only a few weeks; but to Penny it typified all the theaters in New York, and she loved it and felt it was hers.

The unkempt young man seemed completely at home, for he went straight to a wooden table before the empty footlights, picked up a blue-backed manuscript, dropped it again, and leaning against the table, stood talking to a round man whose hair, what little he had, was gray. Penny watched them for a few minutes, and when the young man swung himself into the orchestra pit and went off through the linen-shrouded theater, she decided he had known the correct way to report. So she got timidly out of her chair and went down to the table.

"Good morning," she said, when the plump man looked up at her. "I'm Penny Parrish."

"Oh, yes." He had a benign face with beady black eyes that looked out from under a thatch of white eyebrows, and instinctively, Penny knew he was Martin Goss, one of the best directors on Broadway, and, in spite of his seeming jocularity, one of the hardest taskmasters.

"Oh, yes, Miss Parrish," he repeated. "Nice to have you with us. Uh—er. . . ." He looked around the stage at the scattered people, then motioned to a motherly woman in a too-long black dress who was knitting an olive drab scarf while she talked with an old man who wore an obvious toupee and a gray vandyke beard. "Mrs. Kerston," he called, "will you please take Miss Parrish around and introduce her to the rest of the cast? Miss Parrish is our Drucilla," he explained, when the motherly woman had taken Penny's cold hand in her big warm one. "And Mrs. Kerston is your grand-mother," he added to Penny.

"Oh, how nice." Penny smiled into the kind, comfortable face beside her and felt she had found an ally. Hand in hand they made a tour of the stage, and when they finished, Mrs. Kerston sat down again with her knitting, pulled a chair closer for Penny, and asked:

"Think you can remember them all, right off?"

"I hope so. The tall, handsome man, who has a classic Greek profile is Mr. Thorndyke and will be Miss Ware's husband in the play. The two cute girls are Patricia Falk and Jaunita Warren; the very blond one is Patricia, and the dark one's Jaunita. And the sort or bubbly woman's Miss Fletcher, who will be my mother—though how she'll manage to look sad and brow-beaten is a mystery to me. And my father is Mr. Moore, who looks much too pleasant to be so mean to us both."

"They're actors, my dear," Mrs. Kerston said, leaning over to count her stitches and making a grimace as she knitted off one. "You wouldn't think that the young fellow I introduced to you, Miltern Wilde, the one who is tweaking poor Mr. Cottingham's toupee from behind, could play a hard-boiled reporter better than anyone on Broadway or in the movies. But he can. I saw him do it last winter, in Ticker Tape. He looks like a boy, but just wait until he tears up a scene or two with you and maneuvers you downstage so you have your back to the audience while he steals the applause."

"Will he do that?"

Penny looked at the blond young man whose crisp brushed-back hair waved a little like David's, and who looked enough like David to make her homesick for him.

"That he will, and he's good at it. But here comes Miss Ware," she announced, rolling up her knitting and reaching down for her bag. "And she has our author with her, Grant Simpson, and Josh. Poor Josh."

Penny stooped over for the knitting bag then instinctively stood up. Janice Ware was coming across the stage, speaking to those she knew, and at the sight of her, Penny's heart did its usual little bounce. She was so slender, so burnished gold, so gracious. Every move was controlled but full of meaning; and Penny waited where she was until Miss Ware put an arm around her, kissed her lightly on the cheek, and said, "It's nice to have you back, darling. This is Josh Mac-Donald, our stage manager."

"How do you do?" Penny, still touching shoulders with the star of the play, looked into the bleak gray eyes of the young man she had met at the stage door. "You think you're starting at the top, don't you?" they seemed to say. "Just wait."

He gave her a brief nod before he turned away to follow Miss Ware to the director's table, and Penny was surprised to find people staring at her and to hear Mrs. Kerston murmur:

"I didn't know you knew Miss Ware."

"Yes, I—I do," Penny stammered. "I was in her stock company last summer."

"And I thought you were new at the game." Mrs. Kerston laughed and added slyly, "perhaps you'll be stealing the scenes from Miltern, or from me."

"I am new." Penny was honest in her answer and she took

the heavy hand that grasped the wooden handles of the knitting bag in both of hers. "I've never been in a real play before," she confessed, "and I want to do everything just right. And I can't tell you how grateful I am to you for being so nice to me."

"There, don't worry, child. Theater folk are always jealous of anyone who's a friend of the star. If you ever need any help, you come to me." Mrs. Kerston tucked a lock of hair back into its knot and added, "They're ready for us to start reading now so we'd better go over."

She dragged her chair behind her and Penny, noticing that others were doing it too, reached for hers. The director was still seated at his table with the author, his stage manager, and his star, but he got up to walk around it and to sit on its edge, facing them.

"I see you all know each other," he said, "and I'd like you to meet Mr. Simpson, who has given us what we hope and believe will be a hit." The author half rose from his chair, but as the director was hurrying on with his speech, he stopped a smile of embarrassment and sat back again. "Time for rehearsals is short," Mr. Goss continued, "due to a late spring opening, and I hope we can work quickly together, in good understanding and without too much loss of temper." There was a general ripple of polite laughter, and while he was reaching for his manuscript and arranging for the reading of the first act, Penny looked at Josh MacDonald and wondered why Mrs. Kerston had said, "Poor Josh." He was lounging sidewise on his chair with an arm hooked over its back, and while she regarded him, his eyes flicked up and met hers.

Up Goes the Curtain

She looked quickly away, and when Martin Goss said, "We'll go through the play as we are, reading the parts and getting the picture as a whole," she smoothed the typewritten script on her knee and gave it her full attention.

The morning seemed to last but a minute. All too soon it was one o'clock and they were dismissed for lunch. "Be back at two," the stage manager called, and Penny pushed back her chair. She looked around for Mrs. Kerston, only to see her taking a package of sandwiches from her knitting bag, so started off alone.

"Want to go with us?" the yellow-haired girl called. "Jaunita and I are going to grab a malted milk at the drug store."

"Thanks, I'd love to." Penny was grateful for companionship, but when they were outside Patricia said:

"So Ware's a buddy of yours."

"I just know her." Penny found herself explaining again about her experience in stock, and when she had finished, Jaunita nodded and answered:

"That's all right, then. Acting's like going to school, you know. You have to guard against the teacher's pet. I guess Ware'll take you along in your stride."

"I know she will. She made me earn the part, you see, and I've been trying to get a job all winter." Penny slid onto a stool, wishing she were in Letty's drug store. She would have liked to lean across the counter and tell Letty all about her morning. But an over-rushed girl slapped a dripping malted milk before her, poked out a box of straws and a check, and Penny mopped up the counter with a paper napkin.

"There's Miltern Wilde at the cigarette counter," Patricia said, swinging on her stool toward the front of the store. "He'll make a play for you."

"For me? Why?" Penny looked at the cigarette counter, too, and the other girls shrugged, but Jaunita volunteered:

"Because you're a pal of Ware's. He'll work it for all he's worth, and then stick a knife in your back. So watch out."

"That's silly." Penny started to laugh but Miltern Wilde was already strolling toward them and she felt Jaunita kick her.

"Hello," he said, stopping behind her and still looking as frank and young as David. "About ready to walk back to the grind?"

"Almost." Penny smiled at him then turned to the girls. "Are we?" she asked.

They slid off their stools and, as she paid her check, Penny thought, Everybody in the theater can't be out to cut *someone's* throat. My goodness, it's going to be awful if I have to be on my guard all the time. I'm just not going to believe it!

Miltern Wilde was beside her as she came out onto the sidewalk, and she stepped back so they could walk four abreast. He had a wide mouth and a short nose that went gayly skyward and seemed as happy and inconsequential as the nonsense he chattered. Penny liked him; she liked him even better than she did Patricia or Jaunita who had no small talk to offer except criticism of most of the actors.

"Cottingham quavers," Patricia said as they turned into the alley. "He shakes so I thought his script was going to fly over the footlights. I bet he'll be out in a week."

"Don't fool yourself. He's nervous and slow." Miltern

held back the door that was already as friendly to Penny as the one at home, and went on, "Give the old boy time and, even if the show flops, his rave notices will beat any the rest of us get."

"Not if Ware decides to tangle with him."

The girls went inside and Miltern Wilde winked at Penny and said, "Actors are like monkeys—they're the craziest people."

The afternoon was slower than the morning, and when at six o'clock the cast was dismissed, Penny had walked miles around the stage. She had gone in and out of countless imaginary doors that were gaps between two folding chairs; had poured dozens of pretend-cups of tea; had said her entering line in every conceivable fashion—from inside the room that wasn't a room, from outside it, from half inside and half out; until her feet were burning above the high heels of her pumps and her voice was a hoarse contralto that was unrecognizable to her. She decided on the extravagance of a cab, and was hobbling along the alley, when the dark, dejected stage manager passed her without notice. He walked with an irritated lunge and she wondered why he wasn't in uniform. Miltern Wilde had frankly explained a punctured ear drum, but Josh MacDonald, for all his pale leanness, looked healthy and cross enough to frighten a Jap or a German out of his fox hole. He swung around the corner and Penny limped to the curb where she beckoned vainly for a cab.

It was after seven when she reached home, and when Carrol had propped her up on the divan with a cup of hot tea, she grinned and said feebly, "I'm soft. I can't take it."

"I really didn't think you should wear those shoes but I

hated to say so." Carrol looked at Penny's feet that were now enveloped in red plush mules, and asked, "Was it fun?"

"I don't know. I was scared for my life most of the time. Miss Ware was nice to everybody, just as she always is, but some of the people were queer." Penny sat up and launched into an account of her day that was graphic and ended with, "Mrs. Kerston said to come to her if I ever want to know anything, and sometime I'm going to ask her why that crazy Josh MacDonald acts the way he does. He's plain rude to everyone. And you ought to watch him grab a chair out of your hand when you move something he says is a door. Even if you only shove it an inch."

"Perhaps he's frustrated by life or has a wife he doesn't like."

"Pooh. No girl would marry him."

Carrol laughed at Penny walking stiffly into the dining-room, and said, over the candles and flowers when they were seated across from each other, "David telephoned."

"He *did?*" Penny revived, both from Carrol's words and a taste of soup, and asked, "When's he coming?"

"I couldn't understand what he meant. He kept talking about calling me again when he can, and he said...." Carrol laid her spoon on her plate and went on slowly, "I don't think he's coming, Pen."

"Oh, darling, why not?"

"I think...." Perkins came into the room to remove her untouched soup and she waited until the pantry door had closed behind him again before she said, "I have a feeling they're going straight on, perhaps tonight."

"Oh, surely not."

Up Goes the Curtain

The telephone in the library rang and Carrol sprang from the table and ran through the hall, with Penny's mules clopping along behind her.

"Oh, David, David," Penny heard her say. "Won't I see you again?"

"Don't be worried, sweet." David, somewhere in a telephone booth, kept his voice calm. "I love you, Carrol, always know that. And we'll have our dances together. Later. We'll have all our lives together."

"Yes."

"But I'll have to go now."

"Yes, I know, but ... Oh, David, I love you so. I. ..."

"I love you, too, Carrol, forever and ever. Good-by, now."

"Good-by. Good luck, darling ... good-by."

Carrol dropped the telephone and buried her head in her arms. "I'll be all right in a minute," she sobbed. "It's just—I did expect him to come."

"I know, and it's hard."

"I didn't want him to know I was crying." Carrol lifted her head, and with tears running down her cheeks, asked, "I didn't sound weepy, did I?"

"You sounded better than I could. You sounded swell— even to tossing off a 'good luck.' " Penny gathered Carrol into her arms and vowed silently over the bright head that was pressed against her:

Not for me! I'd let the whole cast stab me in the back and walk on me before I'd go through what she is going through right now.

CHAPTER XI

R EHEARSALS went along rapidly, with Penny spending long hours in the theater. She liked everyone in the cast, was tireless and eager, and would rush home at night to curl up in a chair and tell Carrol the amazing experiences of her day.

"That crazy Miltern Wilde is driving me stark raving mad," she said one evening. "He's fun; we go out to lunch together and he clowns around, but let him set foot on the stage and—wow!"

"What does he do?" Carrol had had a cable that morning, saying David was somewhere and safe, so she leaned back, glad to be entertained by Penny's nonsense.

"Well," Penny thought for a moment and then said doubtfully, "I don't think I can explain it unless you want to stand up and be me, and I'll be Miltern. We have a sort of one-sided love scene," she explained, when they were in position, with her hands on Carrol's shoulders. "He wants to marry me, just for my money, because I'm kind of a shy nitwit," she added with a grin, "though I turn out fine in the last act. But when we get together I'm all frightened and confused. He's supposed to hold me lightly, like this; but he clamps his hands on my shoulders and keeps turning me around until, if I don't brace myself, the first thing I know, the audience will have a swell view of *him* and I'll be wondering if my stocking seams are straight."

Carrol laughed and Penny began a steady pressure that

forced her either to turn or lose her balance. "You see?" Penny said. "It isn't pleasant, is it?"

"It's terrible. What can you do about it?"

"I don't know. I can complain and have everyone think I'm a tattle-tale—Miltern knows I won't do that—or I can have a fight with him about it and look like a cry-baby, or I can just grin and bear it. I don't know yet what I'm going to do, but I'm afraid something's going to happen."

And the next morning it did.

A number of things had gone wrong during the rehearsal. The author had refused to change a line, Mrs. Kerston was talking through a cold in her nose, actors were late for entrances, and the director's temper was short. Penny was halfway through her scene with Miltern Wilde when Mr. Goss knocked the script from the prompter's hand, rushed across the stage and gave her a push.

"Miss Parrish!" he shouted. "Don't stand there like a wooden dummy! Wilde can't play the scene alone. Give him some help. Watch me."

He let Miltern clasp him in his arms (which would have looked ridiculous to Penny had she not been furious with the hands that were gentle on Mr. Goss's padded shoulders) and said, with both shyness and fright, "I wish I could love you . . . but . . . Oh, Denny, I *can't!*"

He used exactly the right tone and Penny knew it. But she also knew that he was standing sturdily on both of his feet. She watched him finish the scene and when he turned to her with a gruff, "Try it," she stepped back into her place but said, "The line is hard for me, Mr. Goss, the way I'm supposed to give it. Would you mind if I try it differently, just once?"

"Go ahead. Give her the cue, Wilde, and go back a few speeches. Go back to, 'I want to make you happy, Drucilla.'"

Penny felt the familiar pressure of hands on her shoulders but it wasn't so heavy now. She even found she could stand quite still to speak, giving the audience a fair view of both their profiles. She knew it was another strategy of Miltern Wilde's and, as she accepted her cue, she began the usual pivot, forcing him now, as he had forced her. She could read his surprise in the way he threw her the lines, and after she said, "I wish I could love you," she pulled away from him, turned, and with her face in her hands, cried brokenly, "But, oh, Denny, I can't."

This left Mr. Wilde with nothing to caress but her back and as he was forced to murmur, "Oh, darling," he instinctively clasped Penny around the waist, bent his head, and finished the scene with her face tipped back against his breast pocket and the audience regarding the part in his hair.

"Good. Go through it again and play it like that." Martin Goss trotted back to his table and Penny let her eyes laugh up at Miltern.

But he bore her no malice. "Touché," he said when they made their exit. "You'll make an actress, yet."

"Thanks." Penny went off to find a chair and to gloat alone over her triumph. She saw Josh MacDonald making notes on a tattered sheet of paper and in her happiness offered him a smile, but he only gave her a nod and went on pacing off the space for a backdrop behind the garden.

"He's a mess, too," she told Carrol that night. "I asked Mrs. Kerston about him and she says he's been sick. It seems he was on the up and up as a director but nobody knows what happened. One day he appeared in Goss's office and got this job as stage manager."

"Was he ever in the army?"

"I don't know." Penny leaned back and yawned and Carrol went over to sit beside her on the divan.

"I saw Letty today," she said.

"You did?" Penny tucked her feet under her and curled up in her corner. "What did she say?"

"I happened to be near the drug store so I went in, but she wasn't there; the manager said she's been sick. He gave me her address and I went to see her. Oh, Penny," Carrol clasped her hands together and shuddered, "I wish you could see that awful place she lives in!"

"Is she very sick?"

"Not now, but she almost had pneumonia. She was propped up on a lumpy iron bed and she hadn't had much to eat, although some girl on her floor has tried to bring some food to her. So . . ." Carrol stopped and looked at Penny. "I asked her to come here and live with us," she said.

"Will she come?" Penny sat up, eager and pleased, but Carrol shook her head.

"I don't know. I told her about the room and bath on the third floor, next to the one Bobby has when he's here, and said she could come and go as she liked. But she's so terribly proud."

"I know she is. But wouldn't it complicate things to have her here?"

"No." Carrol ran her finger along the green silk tufting of the divan. "I doubt if I can make you understand how I feel about Letty," she said. "Having David taken away from me has given me such a lot to think about. So many girls are giving up men they love, and so few of them are as fortunate as I am." She looked about the beautiful room and added slowly, "I have so much. Letty has nothing."

"And so you want to share with her. And you'll make her think she's doing you a favor by coming. You've always been like that, darling."

"But I've never known anyone who has to live as Letty lives. I couldn't be as brave as she is if I had to do it. I want her to have a chance; Joe, too—just as David and I have." Carrol looked at Penny with a wistful, far-away light in her eyes. "David would want me to do it," she said. "He'd say, 'Sweet, you can learn a lot from Letty.' And I can."

"She'll be sort of funny and gay to have around." Penny was eager, now, although a little amused at the disapproval which would show in Perkins's straight back when Letty addressed him with slangy naturalness.

But Carrol was planning seriously. "I found out that the woman where I have my hair done needs a receptionist," she went on. "Someone to write down appointments and to look after people, you know. Letty's pretty and sweet and she ought to have a better job than she has. She could do that, I know."

"Did you tell her about it?"

137

"No, I didn't hear of it until after I'd left her."

"Then let's go over and bring her back tonight. I'll bet, between us, we can do it. Just move her right in."

"All right. And let's spend the gas to have Parker drive us so we can load up her things."

Carrol and Penny jumped up from the divan and a few hours later the most surprised girl in all New York was Letty Brown, who found herself seated in a limousine, her shabby suitcases behind her in the luggage compartment.

"Oh, honestly, I can't do it," she had protested while Penny dumped everything out of her dresser drawers and Carrol laid out her clothes.

"But we need you. Penny's going off to Boston with her play and I'll be alone." Carrol chose a suit for Letty to wear and said from behind the flowered curtain that served as a clothes closet, "You and I can talk about Joe and David, for truly I'll be awfully lonely at night when Penny's play begins."

So Letty had got into the car and docilely let them lead her into the elevator that stopped at the floor of Carrol's triplex apartment; but once in the flowered chintz-done room that was to be hers, she refused to go to bed and sat on a small sofa, looking about her with such joy that the girls were ashamed to watch her.

"I've never thought I'd ever have anything like this again," she said. "Not since Joe and I had the little apartment with a balcony, and I had my own furniture and flowers and a maid to clean sometimes."

"You'll have another one." Carrol sat down beside her and

took her hand. "That's what David and I had, too, and we'll both have it again."

"If I can keep on saving, Joe can own his own business when he comes back. Living here though. . . ."

"Living here you'll save even faster. Penny has no qualms about staying here without paying and you aren't to have, either." And then Carrol told her of the needed receptionist. "The drug store's too hard for you, Letty," she ended, and then added with a smile, "You see, we're planning to run your life for you so you might as well give in. And now, let's have some food sent up. I'm starved."

So life settled down to a steady routine, with Penny rushing off to rehearsals and fittings, and with Carrol and Letty writing their letters or going to a play or a concert on the nights they were alone.

Scenery arrived for *The Robin's Nest*, and the actors learned to walk through real doors and to close them. Penny stood on the stage admiring the set with the others; the thick red rug, the ivory walls and bookcases, the stairway that led to an imaginary upstairs and ended on a wooden platform and steep steps; the terrace with its wicker chairs and pots of flowers, and the backdrop of the sea.

"I love it," she said, turning to whoever might be standing beside her and finding herself extolling the room's praises to Josh MacDonald. "Aren't you thrilled with it?"

"It's okay."

"But you helped design it! Aren't you proud?"

"If it gets a hand, I am. If the critics give it the razz I'll lose my job."

"But everyone likes it. It's perfect."

"Nothing's so perfect that someone can't improve on it. Even your part, big-eyes. Some girl could take your part and do a better job with it than you can,—so don't start counting yourself a hit."

"I don't. Why, I. . . ." Penny's explanation was lost for he had turned and walked away. He doesn't like me, she thought. I wonder why not.

But she forgot Josh MacDonald in the wearing grind of a dress rehearsal. It was to last all night and she arrived at the theater fortified with a thermos of coffee and a two-hour nap.

Nothing was right. Doors stuck and had to be re-hung while the cast waited. Spotlights, meant to portray sunshine, went off when hurrying stagehands fell over their cables. Lamps refused to light, and a bell rang some seconds after Mr. Cottingham had ad libbed loudly, "I *thought* I heard the telephone ring."

"It ought to be a whale of a show," Patricia said to Penny, after wandering around with Jaunita until dawn, waiting to repeat their brief bit in the first act. "If a rotten dress rehearsal is any sign of success, we ought to be a hit. I've never seen worse. Even Ware blew up in her lines."

Penny had watched Janice Ware from a peephole behind the prompter, and now she rose to her defense. "Miss Ware's wonderful," she championed. "My goodness, she hardly gets off the stage for a minute; she carries the whole thing."

"That's what she's paid to do." Jaunita leaned over to gulp

a swallow of Penny's coffee, then took a sandwich from the tray Josh MacDonald was passing. "But Pat's tired so don't pay any attention to her. Ware's okay and she'll pull us through."

"Do we need it?"

"I wouldn't know, but we've all got the jitters. There's the light of your life looking for you."

Miltern Wilde skirted a table that was covered with stage properties: A vase of roses for the second act, a folded newspaper, Christmas-wrapped packages, and a silver tea set. And as Penny looked up he called, "Want to go across the street for some grub? They won't have the stairway back in place for an hour."

"Will it be all right?"

"Sure."

Penny followed him out into the first faint dawn and clung sleepily to his sleeve. "I've never stayed out all night before," she yawned, "and I don't see how we'll ever make the afternoon train to Boston tomorrow."

"You'll be all set and on your toes." He laughed at her and teased her in a condescending but friendly way while they ate their hamburgers, and when the rehearsal was at last over, put her in a cab and said, "Now, I'll take you home. Where do you live?"

Penny gave him the address and was too tired to notice the empty streets and the white milk truck that stood before her door. She was thinking about going straight to sleep so she could finish her packing early enough to enjoy the excitement of being in Grand Central Station with a group of actors; waiting for the manager, who was a florid, busy Mr. Duncan, to shepherd them through the gates and into their own private parlor car.

"It's more exciting than Christmas," she said the next morning, standing in the hall with her luggage, hugging first Carrol then Letty, who, having resigned from the drug store, was resting before she began at the beauty shop. "Do I look sophisticated and sort of bored with it all, like Jaunita and Pat are going to be?"

"You look as if you're having your first glimpse of the circus," Carrol retorted, then turned as Perkins came into the hall to say:

"Major Hayes is on the telephone, madam, and wishes to speak to Miss Penny."

"Oh, my!" Penny dropped the overnight case she clutched, and ran to the telephone. "Hi," she shouted, "I haven't much time to talk because I'm on my way to the train. Where are *you?*"

"At Dix. Want I should come up tonight?"

"Terry, you can't. I'm leaving for Boston."

"Why?"

"For the opening of *The Robin's Nest.*"

"Want I should come to Boston?"

"Oh, dear." Penny looked mildly exasperated, but she sat down and explained carefully, "The play is opening there tomorrow night, Terry, and I'm in a frightful hurry now and wouldn't have time to see you there, even if you could get there, which you can't. Come up next week."

"Don't want I should come to Boston, huh?" Terry grinned slyly to himself, thinking of the plane that was taking off for Mitchell Field in an hour and the forty-eight hour leave he had coming. "Take it easy, lamb-child," he said. "I'll be on hand with the orchids."

"Not orchids! Oh, Terry, *please!*" There was a click, and although Penny clattered the receiver hook wildly, the telephone was quite dead.

"Oh, stop him," she wailed, rushing back into the hall. "I can't bother with him in Boston. I have too much on my mind. I know I'd forget my lines and he'd laugh at me." She grabbed up a toilet case, began her elaborate hugs once more, but Carrol pushed her into the waiting elevator.

"Now, calm down in the taxi," she begged. "I'll call Terry back for you. Just keep your mind on yourself and have a good time."

"I will. Have I got everything? I've forgotten my gloves —oh, I have one on." She crowded in beside her bags, reached past the incoming Perkins and fluttered her hands in frantic gestures of fairwell. "Good-by," she called. "I can't believe this is me."

The elevator doors closed and she leaned back against the wall. "Perkins," she said, feeling delightfully giddy and enjoying the fright her words wrought on his habitually impassive features, "I really think I could faint if I tried to."

CHAPTER XII

Penny thought never, in all her life, would she be happier than she was in the parlor car, sitting between old Mr. Cottingham and the handsome Mr. Thorndyke. Mrs. Kerston was across the aisle with her olive-drab knitting, which had grown to an unbelievable length and would serve some soldier better as a blanket than a scarf. All along the car people were dozing or reading, getting up now and then to sit on the arm of a chair for a bit of theater gossip or a quick political argument, or wandering up to the front where the electricians, Mr. Thorndyke's valet, and Josh were having a bridge game. Miss Ware had gone straight through to the drawing room, and after watching the porter rush by with a table, Penny knew a conference that would result in a rehearsal tomorrow was in progress with Mr. Goss and the author.

The trip to Boston seemed too short to her and the evening in her hotel too long. There was nothing she could do to improve her looks, since she was shampooed until her hair shone and manicured until her nails glistened, so she walked to the theater with Pat and Jaunita and watched Mrs. Harkins press their dresses. Mrs. Harkins, or "Ma," as she preferred to be called, considered herself "of the theatah" and explained from under a frowsy red wig why she had retired from the stage to become a "dresser."

"It's steady pay," she told the girls. "Not just working one week and laid off the next. A good dresser never has to be out of a job. You remember that."

They solemnly promised they would and she assured them as they left, "You three young ladies will never be late for a change while you have Ma Harkins—and you'll never have a wrinkle in your clothes, neither."

"Well, that's something to be grateful for," Penny said, when they were out on the street again. "I only hope Ma Harkins has a long engagement with us. I've never owned one-third of a personal maid before, and I wish we could call her something fancier than 'Ma'."

"We might say Celeste; like Miss Ware's French maid, Felice."

"Or just Harkins," Penny suggested. "That sounds so British. 'Arkins, tike hoff me 'at.'"

But Jaunita shook her head. "If Ma ever gets confused," she giggled, "and if we don't call her loud and often, one of us is apt to hear her cue when she's still in her slip."

So, because she was Ma and nothing else, Mrs. Harkins kept her name, and the girls shared her the next evening and were grateful for her cheerful face and deft hands. It was a trying time. Miss Fletcher indulged in a mild case of hysterics over a lost earring, and actors walked around back-stage, muttering their cues and with a glassy stare, bumping into others, who were in the same mental vacuum. Only Penny stood calmly in the wings awaiting her entrance, and just before she was to go on, Mrs. Kerston upset her equilibrium by telling her she was too young in the business to know how frightened she should be on opening night. After that she proved herself an actress by going to pieces with the others when she was off the stage and by working coolly and intelligently when she was on.

But at last it was over. At last Penny unfolded a newspaper and spread it on a restaurant table. She was crowded into a booth with Patricia, Jaunita, and Terry, and she cried, "This paper says we're a hit! What have the rest of you found?"

"Mine thinks the play's fair and Ware's a wow." Patricia tried to lay her paper over Penny's, and Terry, who was slower at riffling the pages, muttered:

"I can't find a thing."

The four had stayed up all night in order to read the first morning editions, and Terry was enjoying his intimate glimpse of the theater from behind the footlights, although he had hoped to have Penny to himself.

He had arrived back-stage before curtain time, bearing his orchids which composed quite a dazzling bouquet this time; and from the moment the old doorman let him in, had thought how calm and orderly was the army's invasion of a foreign shore compared to the rushing, shouting confusion that marked a company of actors' invasion of Boston. Penny's dressing room was a small place, completely filled by Ma Harkins, and he was forced to present his floral tribute through a crack in the door. The box of roses he carried was for Miss Ware and had a well-rehearsed speech to go with it. But a very young call-boy whisked the box away from him and went along the corridor knocking on doors and shouting, "Overture! Overture!" with less regard for Terry than a general for a private.

So he retired to the wings where he hoped to have a

glimpse of Penny when she came by; but even there, actors made it plain to him that the army was occupying a square foot of space they needed for their pacing. With a sigh he clutched his bit of pasteboard that entitled him to a seat all his own and, treading softly, removed himself to the buzzing expectant throng on the other side of the curtain.

There he sat, watching for Penny's entrance, nudging the man on his right when she appeared, informing him loudly, "I know her." Now and then he grinned to himself and when the curtain fell at the end of the act, pushed his way into the crowded lobby as if he were the producer of the play. He was so busy that when the second act began and Penny was again on view, several soldiers, two officers, and a sergeant in the marines, nudged their neighbors to whisper, "She's army. A fellow we met knows her."

Terry applauded rapturously with the others when the final curtain fell, and hoped that Penny would see him when she was taking her smiling bows. But she looked shy and very serious about it so he crowded his way back-stage again, only to find himself in a mad revelry that was worse than a carnival. Actors filled the stage, hugging each other and rushing about to cry, "You were wonderful!" "The audience did like it; I'm *sure* they did." The director shouted, the stage manager paced, and whole speeches were being rehearsed and revised, while the author who had been pulled from the wings for a brief bit of acclaim, stood in the middle of things like a bewildered crane.

It was some time before Penny spied Terry. He waited in the "garden," as embarrassed as a guest who has come to call on the wrong day, and she rushed through the door and pulled him inside. "Miss Ware," she said, after she had flung herself around his neck with such abandon that Terry knew she was unconscious, "do you remember Terry Hayes?"

"Why, Major Hayes, how nice to see you again, and thank you for my beautiful roses." Janice Ware was the calmest person on the stage and she turned with an easy grace to hold out her hand to Terry. "We really aren't as mad as we seem," she assured him. "Opening nights are always trying, you know, and so many things go wrong. Did we look too bad from out front?"

"I thought it was wonderful. The audience liked it, too. I made it my business to go around and find out."

"I'm glad of that." She closed her eyes in a second's weariness and Terry said quickly, "You should get some rest. Sit down for a bit."

But she only looked up at him and laughed with the gay charm that had carried the tempo of *The Robin's Nest*. "We have some changes to make with poor Mr. Simpson," she said lightly, "but Penny is through until noon tomorrow. Why don't you take the child out and feed her?"

"Right." Terry was only too happy to watch Penny make inroads upon a thick steak, but when he found himself entertaining two hungry and highly-strung strangers, he sat back in his corner of the booth and devoted himself to fanning the flame of their hope until the morning newspapers ignited it into a roaring fire.

"Listen to this," Penny cried excitedly. "One critic says, 'Janice Ware gives a portrayal of a dominant woman that should rank among the all-time high in acting.' And farther on he says, 'Penny Parrish, a newcomer to the stage, proves herself a competent young actress, handling admirably the long role of Drucilla, who is a colorless society girl.' Oh, dear," Penny said glumly, "is that all I did?"

But no one heard her for they were reading aloud, too. "It looks like a sure-fire hit," Terry said at last, when the girls were willing to leave. "And now, let's take our notices and go home."

He paid the check, and when he had them safely in their hotel lobby, he stopped Penny before she entered the elevator with the others. "I'll have to go back this morning," he told her, "and I won't see the New York opening—but I'll be thinking of you."

"Are you hopping off again, Terry?"

"Right away. I'll call Carrol when I get back. Are there any messages you want to send David, in case I should see him?"

Penny's sleepy eyes opened wide and she caught his hand between hers. "Oh, Terry, I'll miss you," she whispered. "I will."

Two tears welled up and she let them spill over while she looked up at him, but he only wiped them away with his finger, then bent over and kissed her lightly. "You're sweet, lamb-child," he said, "and you're tired; so run along and get some sleep."

"But Terry...."

"And you're emotionally stirred up tonight. Don't say you'll marry me and then regret it and worry over it tomorrow. I'll write to you."

His understanding was so great that after he had waved a

gay good-by and gone striding through the lobby, Penny got into the elevator with a sigh of gratitude. She had very nearly capitulated from weariness and the sense of security his presence gave her, and she murmured his name tenderly before she drifted off to sleep. But when the telephone roused her after a four-hour nap she blessed him for being strong enough to let her keep her freedom. Her future was still hers, and she knew she wanted to spend as much of it as she could behind the bright footlights.

The Boston try-out finished three successful nights, playing to packed houses, with small difficulties smoothing out and with the actors settling into their parts. Miltern Wilde respected Penny's ability and had become so easy to work with that her scene with him was one she looked forward to. On the fourth and last night in Boston she thought suddenly of a bit of business they might add, and after the boy had made his usual rounds of "Overture, overture," took one last look at herself in the mirror and dashed out of her door and across the stage to the dressing rooms on the other side.

Her bright blue dress swung around her knees and she tightened her suede belt while her high-heeled slippers tapped across the rough boards. But when she was in the middle of the set, on the thick red carpet, she heard the orchestra begin the familiar strains of The Star-Spangled Banner. Like a well-trained soldier Penny stopped and stood at attention. A stagehand hurried past her but her head was up and she was seeing the Stars and Stripes high above a fort in Tunisia, or above the jungles of New Guinea.

The Robin's Nest was as nothing compared to the meaning of the music that swept through the curtain, and she jumped when a hand pushed her roughly aside and a voice growled:

"Miss Parrish, you may be a rising young star, but you're blocking the way."

Penny threw her head higher but stood her ground while her eyes blazed at Josh MacDonald. "This is my National Anthem," she said through tight lips, "and you just try to move me."

"Then find a less conspicuous spot to do your grandstanding."

The music ended and she whirled to look at him with utter contempt. "When I hear The Star-Spangled Banner," she said slowly and carefully, "I'll stand right wherever I happen to be. Even if it's in the middle of an act. And if you had one ounce of patriotism—you'd get your work finished in time to line up your men out here. The whole cast ought to be here. I will be. Every single night."

"Well, well. Aren't we dramatic!" Josh looked at her and sneered. "The regular army gal. Why don't you join the WACs, Miss Parrish?"

"Because I have a father and brother overseas and have a family to look after, right here at home. Why aren't you doing something since you talk so big?"

The two faced each other, their shoulders squared, and just when Penny clenched her fists to keep from slapping him, he lowered his insolent stare, turned on his heel and walked off.

She stood for moment in the center of the stage, her errand forgotten, then went slowly back to her dressing room.

No one should be so bitter, she thought. No one so young as Josh is. But at least I know now that he hates me because of the army.

CHAPTER XIII

"NEW YORK will be tougher than Boston," Patricia said, standing in Penny's door, "because we could leave Boston if it didn't like us. But we have to *stay* here. At least, we hope to."

"I know it." Penny had been thinking of Letty and Carrol and wondering if they were in their seats yet. I'm kind of shy about acting before people who know me so well, she mused, after Pat had left, but then, it won't be as hard as when Terry was out front because I'm so sure of my lines, now, and of every move I have to make.

She opened her door to listen for the first strains of the National Anthem, and respecting Josh MacDonald's rights to the stage as its manager, stayed, straight and proud, beside her makeup shelf. He came along the hall and saw her standing there, tossed a box of flowers inside onto a chair, and went on with the stack of boxes he was delivering to Miss Ware. Penny wrinkled up her nose at him, pleased that she had proved her intentions to him and vowing to make him observe her nightly, either in her dressing room or in the wings. She wished she could think of ways to cram patriotism down his throat until he burst into a million pieces from such surfeiting, and then was ashamed of herself for being so childish.

She sailed through the first act and was delighted at the smatter of applause that came at her exit. It wasn't the rousing blast that followed Miltern Wilde, nor did her speeches evoke as many laughs as his, but she was satisfied. And when she changed her high-heeled slippers for gold sandals that were but wisps of straps, and lifted her arms for Ma Harkins to slide a long green dress over her head, her heart pumped happily.

The space between the set and the garden wall was narrow, and as she stepped onto the artificial grass, Penny gathered her diaphanous skirts around her. Miltern was already in his place and when she squeezed past him he said across her shoulder:

"Good luck."

"You said that, once." Penny turned to grin at him, but her cue came and she gave the nervous little giggle that belonged with her entrance, and ran in ahead of him.

Miltern Wilde instantly began his scene with everything he could give it, and she understood why he had wished her luck. It was not the smooth performance of Boston that had filled her with confidence. It was the brilliant characterization of a man who traded on a young girl's weakness, who minimized her with every honeyed word he spoke, and who, should she allow it, would leave her no more personality than a well-dressed dummy in a store window.

Penny felt the tension; felt the audience sit up to watch him as it had in the first act. He was stealing the scene as Mrs. Kerston had warned her he would, and she knew that, for one night at least, the scene could belong to him, or to her, but not to them both. The light of battle shone behind Penny's veiled eyes and she answered his challenge. Whatever pace he set she countered. When he cut in too quickly on her line, as if her words were not worth hearing, she let him wait for another cue while she fumbled for speech and twisted her hands. She met his domination of the weak Drucilla with a timidity that was pitiful, and fascinating to watch.

They fought for ten minutes that seemed an eternity and at last came together in the center of the stage. Penny felt his hands upon her shrinking shoulders, light, as Mr. Goss had demanded. But when she reached the line where she began her familiar pivot, his grasp tightened. He held her close to him and pressed his heavy Oxford down on the open toe of her sandal.

Penny gave an involuntary gasp of pain and jerked loose from him. Miltern, who had meant only to hold her immobile as a statue while he stole the rest of the scene, watched her back away and, through the agony of her bruised foot, clasp both hands around her throat. "Oh!" she cried. Then she turned and ran to the door. It was as if the cruelty of Miltern were the cruelty of the man who was forcing Drucilla's love, and the playwright's lines became hers, so that she stopped and flung back at him, "I'd like to love you, Denny —but I can't!"

After that he received her words in a torrent. And even though he followed her, she played no passive love scene with her head against his chest. Penny made every word count for Drucilla, giving the effect of courage in flight; and when at last she eluded Miltern Wilde whose annoyance was very real by now, she went running off into the garden.

The ovation that followed her was thunderous. Someone in the gallery shouted, "Bravo," and Penny stopped with her trembling hands against her burning cheeks.

"Nice, my dear, very nice," Mrs. Kerston said, hugging her; while Mr. Cottingham, leaning on a cane and ready for his entrance, patted her head and spoke sonorously, "You have the fire, child, the divine fire of an actress. My congratulations."

"Thank you."

Penny, frightened at the thought of what Mr. Goss would certainly say, backed away toward her dressing room corridor. She saw Miltern striding in the direction of Miss Ware's door, looking as if he were breathing fire and might go up in flame at any moment. In fear of what she had done to her part she stopped to watch him, and wondered if she should run to Mr. Goss first, promise never to blow up again; or resign. Drucilla was ruined. Penny knew she had ruined her, for now she was not Mr. Simpson's Drucilla, or even Mr. Goss's. People knew she had feelings, long before they were supposed to discover it, and Penny raised her skirt and looked down at the blood on her toes. Her foot had been crushed and no one had seen it; but everyone had crushed Drucilla's pride for the audience to watch while she remained passive until Mr. Simpson told her to stand up for herself. Penny shuddered in misery.

"I guess I'd better find Mr. Goss," she sighed, knowing he was on the other side of the stage. "I can't go on again until I hear the worst."

She began to feel her way behind the backdrop of the sea just as the curtain fell on the second act, and when she came out, like a green mermaid, shivering a little from her dip in the ocean, Mr. Goss and Josh MacDonald were shouting at each other.

Up Goes the Curtain

"I don't care what she did!" Josh yelled, pounding with his fist against a flat. "She brought some life into that stupid doll. I know directing. I know what the kid's been up against with that lousy part. And thrown to a wolf like Wilde, too. You ought to thank her for helping Ware save your show."

"MacDonald, you're fired!"

There was nothing rotund or pleasant about Mr. Goss, now. He was livid because his ability was being questioned by a young nobody who lashed back at him:

"Okay. I've been fired from a bigger job than this—and you know it. But read the papers tomorrow and see who knows acting."

"Oh—please. I'm so sorry." Penny gave a little sob and ran between them. "Keep Josh," she begged. "Jaunita has understudied my part; she can play it tomorrow night. Just let me go."

Martin Goss turned away from her. He collided with a stagehand and shouted, "Get out of my way, you clumsy fool!" then turned back to say so mildly Penny couldn't believe she understood him, "You stay. And you play the part as it was tonight. Wilde won't bother you again—but nobody's going to tell me how to run my business." And with that he walked out onto the stage.

"Josh." Penny sighed and touched his arm. "I wish there were something I could do. Mr. Goss has always liked you so much. Would it help if I talk to Miss Ware about it?"

"Forget it." He scratched his cheek ruefully, then said with a shrug, "As I told Goss, I lost a bigger job than this one, once, and I'll find something else."

"Josh, listen." Penny clutched him frantically. "I have to

change now or I'll be late for the next act—but will you do something for me?"

"What?"

"Will you take me out to supper after the play?"

"What for?" He crossed his arms and slapped one hand against his elbow while he watched her plead with him.

"I don't know just why," she said. "It—it just seems something I want you to do. Won't you, please?"

"Okay. But nowhere fancy. No place where there's dancing and a hullabaloo over the boys in uniform. Understand?"

"All right. No flag-waving."

Penny tried to smile at him but her heart was heavy. She played Drucilla with great feeling during the last act and even smiled when the audience took her to its heart at the end of the play, and was proud when Janice Ware held out a hand to her, the other to Miltern Wilde, and stepped forward with them. But the thought of Josh lay behind her triumph.

She told Carrol and Letty about it while she put on her own clothes and became Penny again, and since they were going home without her, Carrol said,

"You mustn't worry so, pet. It wasn't your fault. You've said yourself, often, that Josh MacDonald is taciturn and queer."

"Yes, I know. But that's because he's unhappy. I've never liked him but he stood up for me and I might find out what's wrong and help him."

"Well," Letty's shrug was expressive, "if you find out anything it'll be a miracle. Joe has a brother like that and we don't know yet what's bothering him. But we'll wait up to hear what you learn."

During the next hour Penny wondered if she would have anything to report. Josh sat across from her in the restaurant he had chosen, one that was surprisingly expensive and where he was known, but offered no information about himself until Penny, in desperation, leaned across the table and asked:

"Josh, why don't you like me?"

"I like you well enough." He toyed with his fork but she persisted.

"You've taken a lot of cracks at me—but we'll skip that—and you made fun of me for being so patriotic. Aren't *you* patriotic, Josh?"

"Some."

Penny was baffled. He met her questions with a rebuff that was like bouncing a ball against a brick wall, but every time they came back at her she was determined to have another try. So she leaned her arms on the table and began again. "When Mr. Goss fired you, you said you'd been fired from a bigger job. Is that what's worrying you?"

"No."

"Were you a director, then?"

"Heavens, no." He leaned back in his chair and laughed so hollowly that Penny looked at him in surprise. "It was the lowest, meanest job I ever had," he said.

"But you said it was big."

"It was."

"Then, what was it, Josh?"

Up Goes the Curtain

With a jerk he scraped back his chair and got up. "Let's get out of here," he said. Then he looked at Penny's plate of half-eaten food, sighed and sat down at the table again. "Go on, and eat," he commanded. "It's late."

Penny obediently took a bite of chicken and dropped her fork on her plate. "Josh, you worry me so," she complained, half in irritation and half in pity. "You've been perfectly horrid to me for weeks. Then tonight you stood up for me and lost your job. Can't you see I wish I could help you?"

"You'd help me more if you'd eat." He sat with his elbows on the table, his face between wide-spread fingers, and Penny took a few more bites before she laid her napkin on the tablecloth.

"All right, pay the check and let's go," she said. "I guess we're both tired."

They walked silently along Fifth Avenue and as they passed a restaurant, three soldiers came out. "One of them looks a little like my brother, David," Penny remarked, turning her head and smiling a little at them.

"More patriotism."

Josh stalked along and, hurrying to keep up with his long stride, Penny urged, "What's wrong with you and the army, Josh? Are you mad because it wouldn't take you?"

"It took me."

Penny caught her lower lip between her teeth, and they had traversed a cross-town block before she tucked her arm through his and asked softly, "What did the army do to you, Josh?"

"It kicked me out."

Up Goes the Curtain

There was only the click of their shoes on the pavement to break the silence, with the far-off rattle of the Third Avenue elevated and the grind of taxis' brakes at street intersections. Josh volunteered nothing more and Penny walked beside him, waiting and afraid to speak, until at last she was forced to say:

"This is where I live, Josh; right here on this corner."

He stood with her under the blue canvas marquee that stretched across the sidewalk, holding his hat in his hand, until Penny suddenly stepped off of the shallow step, slipped her arm through his again, and said, "Let's walk around another block."

They started off with their strides matching and after a few yards he said, "I don't see how I'll ever get rid of your persistence so I suppose I might as well tell you. I didn't want to go into the army. Like a lot of other guys, I was getting somewhere. But I decided it was the only thing to do if we were ever going to get the war won, so I volunteered. That was three years ago.

"I was shipped out to a camp in Texas and I worked like a mule. I had a grand idea of working up to staff sergeant, but one day a second lieutenant got wise to the fact that I'd been a director and shoved me into putting on shows for the soldiers. That wasn't what I'd joined up for, and it wasn't the army; not to me, it wasn't. I brooded about it and bucked everybody and even tried to pull wires. But I found out it *was* the army, all right. There wasn't one darned thing I could do about it, except watch a second lieutenant grow to a captain while I did his lousy little job for him. And then, because I was so mad to be doing for fifty bucks a month what I'd been paid a thousand for, my nerves blew up. They flew in all directions like a busted light bulb."

"And did the army let you out?"

"Oh, no." Josh spoke bitterly and walked a few steps in silence, remembering the months that followed. "The army put me in hospitals. It gave me fine food and medical care. And then, one day, it told me to go home and rest for a year. I got a new classified number, not even an honest 4-F, and when my time's up I'll be yanked back in again, to start the treadmill all over."

"Oh, Josh," Penny hugged his arm closer and said with a shake of her head, "that isn't the army. That was just one bad break you got and one poor officer. Why, if Dad or David had known you then they wouldn't have let it happen to you."

"Little guys like me didn't run to the top high-rankers."

"But it's like tonight. They do. I couldn't have stood up for myself against Mr. Goss; you had to do it for me. Don't you see that?" Penny leaned forward to look into his scowling face, and he gave a grudging consent.

"Maybe," he growled, "but I didn't know anybody."

"You do, now. And even though you can't see it, I think that keeping the soldiers happy is just about as important as fighting."

"Let the girls do it; I want to fight. If I'm called back to the same old job I know I'll blow up all over again." He waved his free arm with a gesture of finality and Penny stopped and pulled him to a halt beside her.

"Do you want to go back in and fight?" she asked. "When your time's up, that is?"

"In six months? I would."

"Then, will you let me fix it? I know a dozen officers who would put you in combat."

He was silent and walking again, and Penny ran a few steps to keep up with him. "Josh," she begged, "let me make the army mean something to you. I've spent all my life in it and I love it. Give me the chance to prove to you how fair it can be. Don't let the whole be ruined by the bit you saw. Please, Josh."

"I don't believe there's a thing you could do."

"You did it for me tonight in your world—I can do it for you, in mine. Let me prove it."

"Okay. When I'm ready you can do your part for me and the army."

"Not in that tone, Josh." Penny held him back, for they were around the corner again. "What you need," she said matter-of-factly, "is to have a look at Letty and Carrol. They're a couple of gals who're keeping their chins up. Come over to lunch tomorrow and meet them."

"I'll have to work tomorrow."

A slow grin spread over his face and Penny thought how interesting he looked when his features smoothed out and little crinkles fanned out from his eyes. "Goss won't fire me," he told her, kicking at the step like a small boy. "He's my best friend, and his bark's worse than his bite. Goss has helped me along since I was a little kid."

"Whew! I'm glad to know that." Penny gave a puff of

relief then glared at him. "I think you're perfectly horrid not to have told me in the first place," she flared. "I've spent the whole evening worrying about you, and..."

"And enjoying it." He watched her mount the step and look down at him. "You know you loved it."

"I suppose so. But for goodness' sake straighten that tie." Penny reached out and gave his wilted piece of fantastically figured silk a pull. "There," she announced with satisfaction. "I've wanted to do that ever since I've known you. Will you take me out tomorrow night?"

"My, you're a forward piece." Josh leaned against the edge of the building, but Penny only yawned suggestively, daintily patting her mouth with the tips of her fingers.

"I'm only trying to sell the army to you," she countered. "And also, I intend to bring you home and turn you over to two other girls who have me backed off the map. Would you like to come?"

"But definitely."

"Then, good night." She held out her hand and added as he took it, "Thank you, Josh."

"And thanks to you, Penny."

He gave her hand a squeeze and swung away, stopping to call back as she stood looking after him, "I'll drop by with all the early editions of the papers and send them up by the doorman."

CHAPTER XIV

As Penny frequently said, the play was "going great guns." She and Miltern Wilde had declared a truce and their scenes together became high lights in a piece which, according to the critics and box office receipts, was due for a long Broadway run. She had her days at home with Carrol now, with the exception of Wednesday and Saturday matinees, and as Josh often dropped in and Letty arrived like a happy tornado at six o'clock, the apartment was full of warm May sunshine and equally bright chatter.

Letters from David came regularly, and Carrol read them over and over with unvarying delight. "What do you say we open Gladstone in June?" she asked one afternoon after she had finished reading one of the thin sheets on which David managed to write so many lines. "Mums and the children will be here then and David says he's already picturing us out in the country."

"It suits me," Penny answered, curled up in the wide window seat and protected from a twenty-story fall by the terrace. "I can commute or stay in town with Letty, and we can come out for week-ends. And *The Robin's Nest* will close for August. That seems a very fashionable thing to do now, and it gives Miss Ware a rest. Me, I don't need any; though it will be fun to whip around outdoors for a month."

So orders were given for the opening of the brick-and-stucco English-type mansion up on the Hudson and Carrol and Penny looked over their last summer's wardrobes. Days flew by, and one evening Penny had her dinner in a restaurant after the matinee, then telephoned home. Miss Turner's excited voice answered her and when Penny asked for Carrol, Miss Turner said in a flutter of words:

"My dear, Letty rushed home at noon and everything has been in such a turmoil. She and Carrol simply dashed out and left me to phone you, without giving me enough numbers to call. I really haven't been able to reach you."

"Where did they go?"

"Why, to the hospital, of course, to get the baby." Miss Turner's voice was so weak and emotional that Penny strained to hear. "Carrol just told me 'we're going to get him now'—Davy, she meant, and off they flew. I do wish Parker would come home to tell me. . . ."

Penny snapped the telephone into place and began dialing again. The hospital line was busy and she waited impatiently, looking down at her wrist-watch and knowing that at this very minute she should be in her dressing room. It seemed a long time before a crisp voice interrupted her questions with, "Just a moment, please. I'll see if Mrs. Parrish is registered," and left her with silence. Penny jiggled the hook, groaned a little from frustrated haste, then dashed out of the telephone booth and ran the short block to the theater.

It was hard to put on her make-up, to wait for her cue; but just before she was to go on, Josh passed by and she clutched his coat lapels. "Keep trying, Josh, will you?" she begged. "And let me know the second you hear."

"Don't worry, I'll get 'em." He gave her a nod and Penny

crossed the grass, stood in the doorway, and began her hesitant opening speech.

The first act passed and she was through with the second, with Josh continually shaking his head, when Letty appeared in her dressing room door, holding a wet umbrella. "It's raining cats and dogs out," she announced calmly, while Penny sat before the bright lights of her make-up shelf and could do nothing but stare. "But Davy got here, anyway."

"Oh, Letty he's *here?* Davy is? *Really?*" Penny jumped up and gave Letty a hug, wet raincoat and all. "Is he cute?" she asked.

"Cute as a bug." Letty sat down on the one chair and added flatly, "But he sure can yell."

"What did he do?"

"He glared at the great big world and opened his mouth and yelled. He fought the nurse who was trying to get him into some clothes and was mad clear through. I think he likes Baby Heaven better," Letty grinned. "And I can't say that I blame him. Gosh, the things they did to the poor kid."

"What sorts of things, Letty?"

"Oh, weighing him, and dressing him, and parting his hair. Who cares at Davy's age what his hair looks like!"

"I wish we could bring him home, right now."

"We can't. The little king's already having a fancy formula concocted and will have expert care behind a glass window until he learns how to manage germs. It's really something," Letty said, shaking her head.

"And what did Carrol say when she saw him."

"She took one look and laughed. 'Letty,' she said, 'he's

even funnier-looking than David said he'd be. He's the most beautiful ugly baby I ever saw.' And that's as long as she got to look at him, either. Whips, he goes. Back into his air-tight nursery."

"Could I see him tonight?"

"Not on your life; not in that hospital." Letty drew herself up and looked at Penny over imaginary glasses. "The nursery window shade is lowered at eight," she said, imitating a floor nurse. "Our babies must have their rest away from prying eyes."

"Then I'll go first thing in the morning." Penny went dancing around the room, holding out her arms and cooing, "Come to Aunt Penny, darling." Then she began to laugh. "Imagine Carrol and David trying to make Davy mind them," she chuckled. "Won't it be a riot? I hope he stands up and socks 'em."

"I think he will. He looks to me like the belligerent type."

However, little Davy, when they brought him home from the hospital, settled down into his nursery with a pleased yawn, and was completely satisfied with the setting life had provided for him. The yellow hair on top of his round pink head was combed into a curl, and his eyes that were the violet-blue of Carrol's, closed contentedly. The girls hung over his crib, resenting the things a starched nurse did for him and longing for the time when he would be completely theirs.

"Letty is going to help me take care of him this summer," Carrol said, when they had tip-toed into her room and she was lying on the chaise longue, with the two relaxed in chairs beside her. "Letty's decided to give up her job and stay home."

"Did you, Letty? That's wonderful of you!" Penny was eager to express her admiration but Letty only answered indignantly:

"Why shouldn't I? Do you think we want some nincompoop to neglect him? He's something special, and we want him in good condition for David to see."

She got up and went back to the nursery for another look and Penny said to Carrol, "She and her Joe will have a different life because of you. I suppose you know that, don't you?"

"I hope so." Carrol looked thoughtfully through the window at the towering buildings in the distance. "Letty talks to me a lot when we're here alone," she said, "and she loves the country. So does Joe. And they hoped, someday, to own a farm. Her father was a farmer, and Joe used to work for him when he was going to school. So I've been thinking about the lodge house at Gladstone."

"But what about the Merrills? They've lived in it and Mr. Merrill has farmed for you for ages."

"He's getting old and they want to leave as soon as the war's over. I talked to Letty about it; and Joe can farm on shares, and can gradually buy the land out of the salary I'll pay him to take care of Gladstone when we aren't there. She's crazy about the idea and wrote a long letter to Joe."

"I hope he wants to do it." Penny listened to Letty in the nursery, then jumped up and ran along the hall when a maid came to tell her Josh was downstairs.

"Come up and see what we have," she called over the banister, softly, so as not to wake the baby.

Josh gave his hat to Perkins and climbed slowly upward. "Don't think you're going to make a nurse out of me," he said, walking along beside her.

He was completely at home with the girls, and while he was often gruff and outspoken, there was nothing sulky about him when he was with them. His temper still flared when he worked and sarcasm bit into his words, but Penny had a way of looking at him that calmed him, and she was forced to admit that his keen suggestions had saved her many mistakes.

There was the day he said to her, "Look. Don't go traipsing across the stage with the sugar bowl for your grandmother. It's awkward, and the audience isn't going to notice if the old lady gets sugar, or not. Skip her, and go back and sit down."

"But Mr. Goss told me to," Penny had argued. "He said specifically...."

"Nuts, to Mr. Goss. He's not up there acting like a fool. Cross left from center and stay there."

So Penny had followed his directions, and no one, not even Mrs. Kerston, had mentioned that one cup of colored water was insipid. Penny was grateful to him, for the simple move had been easier; but many of his suggestions had been directed at her, personally, and made her lips tighten when she remembered them.

There was the night he brought her a note from a Princeton boy whom she knew, and while she read it he lounged against her dressing room door.

"Does he want a date?" he asked.

"Umhum," she answered, laying the note under a picture of Terry and sitting down to begin her make-up. "I'm going dancing tonight."

"Oh, no, you aren't."

Josh came from behind and stared at her in the mirror. Penny wore an old smock, and her hair was pushed back from her face, and covered by a white towel pinned in the back. "See those smudges under your eyes?" he pointed. "You're going home and to bed."

Penny's temper had flared, but eventually she wrote the Princeton boy a note of regret and Josh went off with it. Sometimes he walked her home from the theater because he said she needed the exercise, and often he brought her a glass of milk, which she detested. She fumed at his domination, but had to admit to herself that Josh was the only man she had ever known who continually subjected her will to his, and for her own good. He was completely fair with her, and watched over her only as a comrade who desired to be nothing more. Now, looking at him in the hall, Penny suddenly said:

"I'm going out to Gladstone tomorrow to look things over for Carrol. Would you like to come with me?"

"A rural Friday," he scoffed. "Do we have to?"

"You don't. I just thought you might like to go."

"In the limousine, all fancy?"

Penny stood outside the baby's door and laughed, then dropped her voice to a whisper. "We'll go on the train," she promised, "and you can wear your horrible old clothes and look as awful as you like. You're hopeless, anyway."

She turned into the nursery, not waiting to see if he followed her, and was surprised at the gentle way he held out a finger for Davy's tiny hand to curl around.

"Cute little rascal," he pronounced, loud enough to make Davy's eyelids flutter and the nurse look up from the book she was reading.

"Sh," Penny warned, "do you want to wake him?"

"That was the idea. I wanted to hold him." Josh leaned over the crib to look at the sleeping baby. He moved a blanket nearer Davy's chin and muttered as he followed Penny out, "He ought to be a swell little boy from what I've seen of his family."

"You'll think that even more when you meet his daddy."

Carrol called that she and Letty had moved into her sitting room, and when Penny led Josh in, he went with his arms open.

"Well, well, Mamma," he said, going straight to Carrol and kissing her heartily before he stood back to admire her, "you look young and beautiful."

"And happy," Carrol said gayly. "And thanks for the tons and tons of flowers you've sent me. Davy liked his china elephant with the bachelor buttons in it, too. It looked so mannish."

"It wasn't much." Josh shrugged and added, "I tried to find him an electric train, but they aren't making them, now."

The girls laughed at him and he said defensively, "Well, it's fun to play with. My father had an electric train when I was a little boy, and the hardest licking he ever gave me was because I tried to turn the switch when he and Martin Goss were putting in some new track."

"Did Mr. Goss ever play with trains?" Penny asked, unable to visualize the rotund director down on the floor, on his hands and knees.

"He played with mine." Josh grinned around the room then suggested to Penny, "How about going to Hardi's to dinner? I have some ideas I want to talk to you about."

"All right." Penny got up, hating to leave home and the new member of the family. "You won't be lonesome, will you?" she asked Carrol, "if Letty has to go out to Jamaica to tell Joe's family good-by?"

"I'm going to write to David and take care of Davy, all by myself. In fact, I can hardly wait to begin."

She saw them off from the head of the stairs, then gathered up her writing portfolio and crossed the hall. For the first time she felt like Davy's mother, and the exquisite thrill made her hands tremble as she raised the shade a little. The nurse had gone down to her dinner and Carrol leaned over her son, letting her eyes feast on each tiny feature. "Your daddy and I love you," she told him softly, "better than anything else in the world. You're our own little boy."

Davy lay on his side and his eyes remained closed, but his mouth moved a little as if he were telling her how pleased he was to be there, and Carrol smiled at him, then went to a cream-and-white painted chest in a corner. She opened a drawer and took the pink silk bonnet from its nest of tissue paper, holding it on her fist and turning it from side to side. Davy still slept so peacefully that after a few seconds she tip-toed back to him again. With a swift deft motion she turned him onto his back, lifted his head, and slipped the bonnet over it. Then she laid him down again and tucked the ribbons under the fat roll of his chin, and stood off to admire him. Little grunts of dreams came through Davy's lips and she let him enjoy them, putting the bonnet away and sitting down by the window to begin her letter.

For some time her pen scratched steadily, until, unable to wait longer for the telling, she wrote:

"Oh, David, darling, Davy wore his pink silk bonnet just now, and I could see that he's going to be just as handsome and wonderful as you are!"

CHAPTER XV

PENNY and Josh arrived at Gladstone in a taxi. They swept around the semi-circular drive and alighted before the wide brick terrace; and after he had paid the driver, Josh gave a low whistle.

"Poor little Davy Parrish," he said, following Penny to a window where she was trying to peep through a knothole in a heavy wooden shutter. "The poor little rich boy."

"Not Davy," Penny said, dusting off her hands. "Carrol and David do a lot of good with the money and they've lived on David's pay ever since they've been married." She sniffed the flower-scented air and suggested, "Let's walk around the grounds while we wait for Mr. Merrill to come and open up for us. You're always wanting me to walk and this country air's good to take the city's gasoline fumes out of our lungs."

He turned beside her and walked across the green lawn, swinging a small basket of lunch they had brought, and Penny said reminiscently, "I had a wonderful time living here when Carrol's father was alive. He did everything he could to make us happy when Dad went over to England."

They passed the tennis courts where once lawn furniture and gay umbrellas had made bright color through the trees, and under a giant oak that stood like a sentinal between the lawn and the woods, Penny suddenly stopped. "Let's sit here and talk," she suggested, dropping down on the grass without waiting for his answer. "I'm hungry; aren't you?"

Josh grunted that he was, and she opened the little wicker

hamper and brought out sandwiches. He was silent while he sat munching, and Penny went on companionably talking to herself. "There's a lane over there that leads to the stables, and Carrol and Uncle Lang and I used to ride every day. I had a beautiful horse named Martinette, and we'd go galloping over the meadows." She turned her head and asked idly, "Do you like to ride, Josh?"

"On a merry-go-round. I've never tried anything else."

"I like merry-go-rounds, too." Penny slid farther down against the tree trunk and prodded with sudden interest. "What else do you like?"

"Walking in the rain."

"I do, too."

"With an old felt hat pulled down over my eyes and watching the drops spatter on the pavement."

"I like it beating against my face and to hear it dripping from the trees, and to have a dog pattering along beside me, snuffling at the wet leaves."

"I never had a dog." Josh reached for a sandwich, and as she handed him one, Penny asked:

"Wouldn't your parents let you have a dog, or didn't you want it?"

"Oh, I wanted it, all right; what boy doesn't?" He rested on one elbow, stretched out, and said as if she wouldn't understand. "I belonged to the class of kids who doesn't get what they want. You wouldn't know that class, Penny."

"But I would," she insisted. "You and I like the same things: the stage, the rain, dogs, and reaching for the brass ring on the merry-go-round. Children are all very much alike. And if they grow up remembering, trying to get the gold ring, but remembering how smooth and brignt the brass one was, they understand each other. Tell me about your boyhood, Josh."

"There isn't much to tell." He rolled over onto his back and with his head pillowed on his crossed arms, stared up into the leafy branches above him. "Mom was a dancer in a vaudeville act and Pop was the manager," he said. "She lost out after I was born and always blamed me for it, because Pop went right on managing the company, and she and I had to stay home. She was sick most of the time and I don't remember much about it, except that I was always looking out of the window because she never felt like taking me anywhere. And when I was about six she died."

"Oh."

"After that I went with Pop. He had me in and out of almost every school in the country, and when he was flush I went to the best military academies, and when he was short of cash people took me to board; and once, I got in an orphan asylum. That was after he and Goss began producing road shows."

"Were they partners?" Penny asked.

"Sometimes. They'd get together and do a show on a shoestring, and if it succeeded, Pop would rent a furnished apartment in a hotel, send me off to school, and live high for awhile. Then they'd pick a flop, and I'd come home until he found a job as manager of something."

"I don't see how you ever knew what you were doing," Penny said softly.

"I didn't. I felt insecure. That's what psychologists say about children who are bounced around nowadays."

"But, did your father love you?"

"Yes, I guess he did. He hung onto me, at any rate. And one of the best memories I have is of one summer when he took me up to Canada, fishing. He had a flashy yellow car that year and we did the thing up right." Josh laughed a little, remembering. "We had all the dude togs and finest rods he could buy; and when he didn't catch anything he'd yell at the guide to pack up our canoe, and on we'd paddle. He was patient, though, when I got poison ivy."

Penny laughed with him and asked, "How old were you then?"

"I don't know; eleven, I guess. Pop had registered me in a boys' school for that fall, but something went wrong, and that's when I ended up in the orphan asylum—only it had a fancier name. It was called The Good Shepherd's Home for Lost Lambs. Pop thought it sounded dramatic and paid them a little something to take me." Josh ruffled up his hair and said thoughtfully and with wonder, "You know, that was one of the best places I hit. I think I'll send 'em some money sometime. By George, I will."

He became lost in memories of The Good Shepherd's Home, and Penny poured him a cup of coffee and wriggled over to him. "What else did you do?" she asked, on her knees, watching him drink it.

"Well," Josh handed back the cup and grinned at her. "You're a curious kid, aren't you?" he asked.

"No, I'm not." Penny shook her head solemnly. "I'm just finding out why you're so cross and untrusting sometimes, and why the army frazzled your nerves."

"I was frazzled to start with." He lay back on his arms again, and Penny sat facing him.

"Go on," she prompted.

"Well, Pop eventually retrieved me from the Home and we went up and down like a see-saw. Goss had got smart by then and was making a name for himself as a director, and the winter I was sixteen, he took us in for awhile. Pop found a job, managing a company that was going to South America, so he left me there—and after a couple of years wrote me that he'd married a Spanish senorita and owned a night club. He even sent me money for college."

"Did you go, Josh?"

"I'd been in college a year on Goss's money," he answered, "but I didn't stay. I took what Pop sent and looked for a job. At first I had small parts acting, and then I bluffed my way into directing, and with Goss's help at night, did a fair job."

"Do you always call Mr. Goss, 'Goss?' " Penny interrupted. "It sounds so funny."

Josh looked at her without smiling, his eyes that usually scowled surprised into tenderness. "I call him, 'Uncle Dad,' " he said, "when we're at home, but not in public."

"Then you love him, don't you?"

"Uncle Dad?" Josh shook his head with a smile. "The sun rises and sets in him, that's all," he answered.

Penny settled down more firmly into the grass, tucking her feet under her. "That's why you weren't worried about being fired," she said. "Wasn't it?"

"I knew he'd call me up to come over. He's married now

and I have my own apartment; but I like his wife, and she doesn't mind how much we fight or how loud we yell. And we yelled at each other plenty, that night, over you."

Penny laid the palms of her hands flat on the ground and leaned forward on her arms, one shoulder supporting her cheek. "Why did you fight over me?"

"Because I think you have the making of a great actress— if you aren't ruined. And I expect to manage you and direct the play you star in."

"Oh, Josh!" Penny stared at him in unbelieving surprise, but he only lay on his back and met her excited eyes with a scowl.

"I doubt if you'll like the things I'll make you do," he said. "You're hard to handle."

"What sorts of things?" Penny's voice was a whisper, but he answered in a calm, even tone that was almost sing-song. "Rest, exercise, study, and the constant search for improvement. If you want to be a success *you can't let down for one minute in one show.*" He was silent after that, reading the changing emotions in her eyes above him, until at last he said, "And, of course, there's marriage."

"Marriage?" Penny swallowed, then asked, "Couldn't I marry?"

He shook his head. "Not Major Hayes or any of the boys you fritter away your time on. If you should, you can't belong to the theater, Penny. You can't live in two worlds."

"Oh." Penny sat back and stared down at her shoe. "Not being in the army wouldn't matter so much if. . . . Do you really think I'll be as great as Miss Ware, someday?" she murmured.

"You'll be better—if you don't get sidetracked." He pushed himself up and fumbled in his pocket for a cigarette, while Penny, still without looking at him, asked:

"How old are you, Josh?"

"A great deal older than you, my child." He struck a match and said over its flare, "When I was fishing in the Canadian woods with Pop you were a baby in your basinette."

"Have you ever been in love?"

"Once, but it didn't take. The lady didn't like my being a private in the army."

Penny looked up then, but he blew out a cloud of smoke and grinned at her. "I heard a car come in," he said. "Don't you think we should hunt up the caretaker and get started home as soon as we can?"

"I suppose so."

She got up and began cramming waxed paper back into the basket. Josh sat where he was, watching her while she carefully put the lid on the thermos and dropped it in beside the paper. When she had everything ready, he ground out his cigarette and sprang lightly to his feet.

"Army setting-up exercises," he said cheerfully, not noticing her preoccupation.

He let her carry the basket and when they were almost back to the house she stopped to ask, "Could we go to Coney Island some Sunday night and ride on the merry-go-round?"

"We might."

"Would you try to get me a ring? A gold one?"

"I'd try, but I doubt if I'd do it; I never have, yet."

He walked on and as Penny caught up with him, she heard

183

the telephone ringing. Mr. Merrill's rattletrap car stood in the driveway and the front door had been unlocked, so she ran inside. She stumbled through the unaccustomed gloom of the hall and into the dark library, snatching up the receiver. "Hello," she said, feeling around for a chair.

"Oh, Penny," a worried voice answered, "this is Carrol. I hated to have to call you but—oh, dear."

"What is it? What's happened?"

"Oh, Penny, Mrs. Drayton phoned . . . Michael's mother . . . and she said. . . ."

"Has something happened to Mike?"

"His plane was shot down over Germany and the War Department just notified her. It said, 'missing in—action.' "

"Then I'll bet he's a prisoner." Penny tried to be hopeful but was glad for the chair she finally located. "Did he bail out?"

"She doesn't know. She's over on Governors Island and wants you to call her as soon as you can. She thought David might find out something for her, and I'm trying to get a cable through to him. Will you call her, Penny?"

"Yes, right away."

Penny laid down the telephone and sat with her face in her hands. Michael. How many times he had been in this room; how many times he had teased David, saying, "I'll be roaring through the sky when you're crawling along in a tank." Dear Michael.

She was still sitting in the dark when Josh came in. "What is it, Penny?" he asked. "Bad news?"

She tried to tell him, but the tears welled up and while she dialed the New York operator she took off her bracelet that

184

had a flat pendant disk hanging from the chain and gave it to him. He snapped the case open, and with the light from a match, looked briefly at a dark-tanned face under an aviator's helmet, at keen dark eyes and a flashing white smile.

"He's all right, Penny," he said. "I don't doubt he bailed out. Tell his mother he has a good chance to make his way into a neutral country. That's what lots of 'em do."

"I will." Penny talked as comfortingly as she could to Michael's mother, and Josh went outside to sit on the steps beside deaf Mr. Merrill and ask about his crops.

They were shouting at each other when Penny came out, and as she stood in the door, dabbing at her eyes with the back of her hand, Josh got up and pulled a handkerchief from his breast pocket.

"Here," he said, watching to see that she did a thorough job of wiping off the streaks her tears had made. "Let's get this job done and shove off."

"You haven't any heart at all," Penny muttered, following Mr. Merrill to the kitchen to look at the plumbing.

"It isn't a question of heart." Josh ran his finger under a leaking faucet and went on, quite sure Mr. Merrill was unable to hear. "You have to work tonight. You can't do it if you destroy yourself emotionally."

" 'Destroy myself emotionally.' Of all the stupid, selfish remarks!" Penny threw back her head and spoke so violently that he turned around and looked at her. "I love Michael!"

"I thought it was Hayes," he answered.

"It's—it's both of them." She watched him pointing out the defect to the old man, and cried suddenly, "Oh, you're such a—such a dope! And cold and hard and—hard."

Up Goes the Curtain

"I was very pathetic to you a little while ago." Josh squatted down and reached through a door to feel the inner plumbing of the sink. "You were quite sentimental about me."

"I was not." Penny watched Mr. Merrill produce a wrench from the hip pocket of his overalls, then rushed from the room. She hurried through the house without seeing what she had come to check, and when Josh walked into the hall to tell her the caretaker had gone for the station wagon, she stood with her lips clamped together, waiting, until she heard tires scrape on the gravel.

"Do you want to drive?" she asked, economical with her words, when the house had been locked and several empty trunks, that would bring back Davy's belongings, had been stacked in the car.

"You do it. It'll be good for you. Calm your nerves."

Josh got into the station wagon and as she went around the back and slid in beside him, Penny tried not to give him so much as a glance. But she knew he was stretched out with his head against the brown leather seat and could hear his fingers tapping tunes against the frame of the door. Conflict raged within her, and it was some time before her anger melted and, like ice in a spring thaw, flowed off and away.

"I'm sorry, Josh," she said suddenly, "for the things I said about you."

"Forget it." He sat up and patted her fingers that were gripped around the wheel. "I don't blame you for being jumpy," he told her, "or for crying over Michael. Tears are good for you sometimes, but there's no sense in getting hysterical. You don't help Michael that way and it's better to know that, since he wasn't killed, he's safe."

Penny swallowed a few times, took a deep breath, and they drove on in silence. They were on the Cross County Parkway when Josh leaned over to look at her and to ask:

"Are you calmed down, now?"

"Yes."

"Then stop the car and I'll drive."

Penny slowed obediently and as they changed places, he said, "It's too late, now, to go by your apartment. I'll let you out at the theater and park in a garage, then I'll have some dinner sent in to you."

"All right." Penny sank back in her corner of the seat and watched him guide them in and out of traffic. He whistled steadily, and once he took his hand from the wheel to reach out and pat her knee, but the rest of the time he confined his remarks to cars that had no respect for his horn which shattered the silence loudly and often.

Lights were glowing along the Hendrik Hudson drive when they entered New York, with windows of tall buildings twinkling like diamonds in the dusk, and he leaned out to look at them. "New York," he breathed. "The greatest living city in the world. Take a look, Penny; it's all yours if you want it."

"I wonder if I do." Penny sat forward and stared up through the windshield. "It's such a big place to want, Josh. Just look at it—so many stars to wish for."

"Only one." He followed the line of cars downtown and said when they stopped before the theater, "There's your star up there. It's the sign that says '*The Robin's Nest*' and has Janice Ware's name under it. Want one like that, Penny?"

"Yes." Penny got out of the car and stood on the sidewalk looking at the sign until she felt him take her arm and lead her into the alley. "I want it," she said, half to herself, "but I want what Carrol has, too; a David and a little Davy."

"You'll have it all, in time." He held the door for her, and when she was safely inside, like an ant in its busy hill or a goddess on her mount, he hurried off.

Penny took her key from the call board and walked across the lighted stage smiling at people as she passed. But alone in her dressing room, she sat down on a hard chair and stared at the wall. The bangle on her bracelet glittered in the bright light and she opened the disk to look at Michael's face. "Dear Michael," she murmured, trying to bring him closer to her and to feel his presence. Her supper came on a tray and she laid Michael's picture beside her plate, smiling a little at the frugal meal Josh had allowed her. But Michael stayed dim and far away in the past, and she could only listen to voices and laughter in dressing rooms around her; until, with her food scarcely touched, she pushed back the table, slipped off her dress and into her old smock.

She laid the bracelet on her make-up shelf beside the picture of Terry and stood back to look at them. She loved them both: she knew that, but how? And which did she love more?

Josh's quick footsteps lunged at the rough boards in the corridor, and without stopping to reason further, she rushed over and flung open the door. "Josh?" she called.

"Yeah?" He stopped and looked back at her inquiringly but Penny only shook her head.

"Nothing," she said. "I only wanted to thank you for my supper."

"Okay. Make it snappy."

Without a word she closed the door again and picked up her white towel. With it half-covering her hair she stopped and stared at herself in the mirror. Footsteps were coming back along the hall and her brown eyes lighted up. The footsteps went on past and she pinned the towel into place and sat down.

"Oh, well," she sighed, dipping her fingers into the cold cream and changing Penny Parrish into Drucilla. "It doesn't matter about me—the show must go on."